MONSTER ACADEMY

MONSTER ACADEMY

CATHERINE BANKS

Crescent Sea
PUBLISHING

Monster Academy by Catherine Banks.

Copyright © 2020 Catherine Banks. All rights reserved.

Published by Crescent Sea Publishing.
www.crescentseapublishing.com

Cover design by Story Wrappers.
www.storywrappers.com

Interior design by Turbo Kitten Industries™.

www.catherinebanks.com

For Cassie and Ashleigh. Thank you for your support and for becoming my friends.

CONTENTS

Chapter 1   1
Chapter 2   11
Chapter 3   19
Chapter 4   25
Chapter 5   33
Chapter 6   41
Chapter 7   49
Chapter 8   57
Chapter 9   65
Chapter 10   73
Chapter 11   81
Chapter 12   89
Chapter 13   95
Chapter 14   103
Chapter 15   109
Chapter 16   117
Chapter 17   125
Chapter 18   133
Chapter 19   141
Chapter 20   147
Chapter 21   153
Chapter 22   161
Chapter 23   169
Chapter 24   175
Chapter 25   181
Chapter 26   187
Chapter 27   193
Chapter 28   199
Chapter 29   203
Chapter 30   209
Chapter 31   215

Chapter 32   221
Chapter 33   225
Chapter 34   231
Chapter 35   235
Chapter 36   241
Chapter 37   247
Chapter 38   253
Chapter 39   259
Chapter 40   267
Chapter 41   275
Chapter 42   281
Epilogue   289
Acknowledgments   293
About the Author   295

MORE BOOKS YOU'LL LOVE
The Siren Wars by K.M. Robinson   299
Midnight by Melanie Gilbert   301

More From Catherine Banks   303

MONSTER ACADEMY

USA TODAY BESTSELLING AUTHOR

CATHERINE BANKS

ONE

FRANCES

The auditorium buzzed with the anxious chatter of over five hundred paranormal teenage creatures waiting for the speeches of elite monsters, and then our first night of school to begin.

Loralie and Tsukiko sat on either side of me. My two best friends wore bored expressions as they slouched in their seats, but I could see the nervousness in the way they clenched their jaws and narrowed their eyes at anyone who looked our way.

I repressed a smirk that threatened to surface.

They were both frustrated at having their grandfathers give speeches to the entire Academy and knowing that, like every year, their doting grandfathers would point them out.

"Stop smirking," Tsukiko grumbled, her amber eyes narrowing, her wolfen ears flat to her head, and her tail swishing behind her.

"I'm not smirking," I lied.

Loralie rolled her eyes. "You always smirk before the speeches because you know we hate them."

"You only hate getting singled out," I corrected her.

"Well, you're about to experience it yourself," Tsukiko said, a slight tilt to one side of her lips betraying her amusement.

My eyes narrowed now. "What do you mean?"

At the front of the large auditorium, on the large stage, a woman in flowing robes smacked her staff on the ground. The boom echoed, and as the sound of it faded, so did the conversation of the students.

"Welcome. For many of you, this is your first year as a high schooler, and your first year at the Northern Territory Academy. We welcome you into our fold and look forward to seeing your academic progress," she said, smiling brightly.

Warmth radiated from her and eased the tension in everyone's shoulders.

Magic.

Like most of the other students, we had gone to the elementary academy for kindergarten through eighth grade. Now that we were in ninth grade, we had been moved to the high school academy. They felt it was better for the development of our minds and social skills to separate us in such a way.

My dad thought it was stupid and we should just have one big school together.

Mom said it was likely due to budgeting and security issues.

I could understand the security issues. As we grew older, the possibility of damaging and seriously harming one another grew quickly. Just an hour ago, I had seen one student toss another into the stone wall, knocking a huge dent in it and causing several stones to fall out.

A witch had gone and reversed the damage, but that was just one incident. If there was a large fight, it might not be cleaned up so easily.

I wished we could combine schools with the other territories, but they claimed there were too many of us and that keeping us separated by territory was easier.

"For those who do not know, I am Headmistress Selene Gonzalez, leader of the Black Cauldron Witches. There are many teachers on staff this year, including some new ones, but first, let's hear from one of our esteemed Council Members, Albus Reaper." She clapped her hands as she stepped away from the podium, and we clapped with her.

Floating up to the stage in full reaper regalia, including the long, black cape, and carrying his scythe, Loralie's grandfather stepped up to the podium. With a flourish, he flipped back his hood, revealing his smiling face. "Good morning, students!" He yelled.

Loralie groaned.

"Good morning, Council Member!" Every student responded.

"This is going to be a great year here at Monster Academy, I can just feel it!" He said with a bright smile. He looked around the room until his eyes landed on Loralie who tried to sink farther in her seat. "My granddaughter is here for her first year, so I'd appreciate you all helping her when you can. She's a good girl, but can sometimes be a bit thick-headed." Albus leaned forward and whispered, "She gets that from her father." He straightened and waved at Loralie. "Wave, dear."

Loralie groaned, but raised her hand and gave a single wave before putting her hands in her armpits.

"Remember, to succeed, we must stick together. Through death and after!" he yelled.

"Through death and after," Loralie muttered. It was their family motto and one she was required to repeat if another member said it.

Headmistress Gonzalez returned to the podium. "Thank you, Council Member. Now, for our next speaker, we have Council Member Kenta Okami!" She clapped her hands again and we clapped, too.

Stalking across the stage in his half-wolf, half-man form, Tsukiko's grandfather looked downright terrifying. Once at the podium, he turned and faced the crowd, his lips pulling back into a snarl. Then, he let his tongue loll out the side of his mouth and he yipped loudly.

Tsukiko groaned and put her face in her hands.

With a few bone popping snaps echoing around the room, Kenta shifted his head into his human one. "Good morning, students!" he yelled, his tail wagging behind him.

"Good morning, Council Member," we replied, but there were a few snickering students behind us.

"Dammit. Dammit. Dammit," Tsukiko muttered.

"This year you will be put under a lot of stress, but you need to remember to have fun as well as work hard. Just look at my granddaughter, Tsukiko, and her best friends, Loralie and Frances, if you need to find monsters who are great at balancing working hard and playing hard. Girls! Raise your hands!"

Flies on feces!

The three of us hesitated too long, and Kenta snapped his teeth.

Our hands shot into the air, and we swallowed hard.

He might have looked sweet standing in front of the crowd, but he could be absolutely terrifying, and he did not hold back when he punished you.

He smiled. "There they are. Now, I want you all to remember to play hard and work hard in equal measures, okay?"

"Yes, Council Member!" Every student replied.

"Must be nice to be an elite," a voice said from somewhere behind us.

"I bet they don't work nearly as hard as the rest of us," another person said.

Tsukiko growled, and Loralie started seeping black smoke.

I set a hand on each of them. "Ignore the idiots. We all know the truth."

Although we had dealt with these same things in the past, we all knew high school would be different.

"Sheep," Tsukiko snarled. "They're all sheep who can't think for themselves."

There was no point in arguing with her or trying to convince her not everyone was bad. She would growl for a bit, but once we got into the classes, she would calm down.

"Why did I get lumped in with you this time?" I asked. "Did you convince Kenta to do that?"

Tsukiko gave me a look conveying how stupid I sounded. "You think I can convince Grandfather to do anything?"

I sighed. "Right." Kenta was known for being super opinionated and not changing his mind once it was made up.

A couple teachers gave speeches, but a fiery head drew my attention, dulling out the sound of everything else.

Two rows in front of us, seven chairs to the left, sat Dante. His hair, literally made of fire, wafted in the breeze, but mainly stayed in the style he picked. He controlled the fire, so he could turn the flames into any style he wanted. One time last year, he'd made it a Mohawk. It looked really cool.

"You're drooling," Loralie whispered in my ear.

I snapped my jaw closed and ran a hand over my mouth, which was completely dry. "Am not."

She snickered.

"Which one has your attention?" Tsukiko asked, looking in the direction I had been.

"Oh, come on!" Loralie groaned. "Him, again? I thought you got over your crush on him year before last? You know you can barely stand near him or talk to him. How do you think you'll be able to have a relationship if you just freak out when he comes near you?"

"I don't freak out when he's near me," I muttered.

She arched a brow. "Really? So, you didn't scramble away from him when you almost got put on his team in PE last year?"

"No," I lied.

She scoffed and rolled her eyes. "Okay, just remember that I warned you to crush on someone else. You're going to crush and then have your heart broken when you realize, again, that you can't be with him."

I mouthed back her words in a mocking way, which earned me a smack on the arm.

"This concludes our commencement ceremonies. Please head to the field and get in line to get your schedules. Welcome to Monster Academy!" Headmistress Gonzalez clapped her hands and rainbow sparks danced across the ceiling before falling on us.

Loralie groaned. "She threw glitter on us? This crap is never going to come out."

I suppressed a laugh as I stood and waited for our row to exit the room. My gaze landed on Dante again and I'd swear for a moment, it looked like he was glancing at me out of the corner of his eye, too.

No, that couldn't be. Definitely not.

"Let's go," Loralie said and nudged my back. "Time to stand in line for an hour and find out if I was able to convince my dad to get us in the same classes or not."

"I think you did," Tsukiko said. "He was very excited at the thought of us being in the same classes to spark friendly competition for top score."

Loralie groaned. "Yeah, he only cares about me being top of the class."

"I heard he made a bet with someone that you would get the highest grade. So, you better not make him lose money," I teased.

She groaned louder.

We shuffled out, Tsukiko holding my left hand, while Loralie held my right hand, ensuring we didn't get separated by the crowd.

We made it halfway out with no problems. Then, Rathik slid in front of us and turned around to smile at Tsukiko.

Rathik was a naga, a snake person, and he'd been trying to get Tsukiko to talk to him for two years now. He could change his lower body into a snake or keep human legs, but had scales along his arms and a few on his throat as well. We'd heard it was because he was worried about being attacked and kept the scales to make it harder for his skin to be pierced by a blade. His darker tone made his scales even shinier in comparison.

"Hi, Tsukiko," he said with his eyes shining.

She tensed, her tail puffing up in shock behind her. "Hi," she breathed.

Loralie pushed past me and smiled up at him. "Your scales are different this year," she noted.

Tsukiko took a small step back, her ears lowered, but her eyes completely focused on Rathik.

Loralie was right, his scales were a brighter green this year, almost neon.

"Thanks, I finally unlocked some new abilities and powers," he said proudly, his eyes moving to Tsukiko several times.

"Rathik!" Someone yelled up ahead.

"I have to meet up with my roommates. I'll see you later?" He looked at Tsukiko, his attention on her fully.

She nodded twice while biting her bottom lip.

He smiled and it was almost blinding. "Awesome. Bye."

He weaved his way through the crowd to meet back up with his friends.

"Oh, I'm the one with an unrealistic crush?" I asked.

Loralie sighed. "You two are hopeless."

I slung my arm around her and smiled. "And you love us."

She looked down at my arm. "Your stitch popped."

Craning my head, I let out a long sigh when I saw she was right.

"Dammit. Well, let's hope none of the others pop until I can go see Dr. Frankenstein and get it fixed," I said.

"She freaks me out," Loralie whispered.

"It's because she's human," I said.

"Or, it's because the woman was granted immortality, and Loralie knows she can't reap her soul," Tsukiko said, finally coming back to her regular self now that Rathik was far away.

"It's not right," Loralie snapped, black smoke seeping from her fingertips and nostrils. "Humans are supposed to die. Preferably quickly."

"They keep elongating their lifespans," Tsukiko said. "It's worrisome."

"They also keep gaining more and more technological advancements. I heard that they developed a flying machine with a camera attached to it. Someone said it almost made it to the school's barrier," I whispered to them.

"They're trying to find our hiding places," Tsukiko said, her tail tucking around her leg. "What happens when they do?"

"They'll never find us," I assured her and hugged her against my side. She was at least a foot shorter than me and fit beneath my arm easily. "If they do find us, we'll kill them and make examples of them like our grandfathers did hundreds of years ago."

Tsukiko smiled, revealing her fangs, and said, "Except we'll be much more brutally efficient."

"Brutally," I agreed with a nod.

"Can't we take a nap first or something?" I grumbled as Tsukiko, Frances, and I got into line to pick up our class schedules.

The lines were even longer than usual this year. That was to be expected with all of the high school-aged creatures coming to Monster Academy. We were always separated at different elementary schools based on territory, but there was only one Monster Academy for high school on this continent.

"We are totally binging some shows after classes," Frances said with a nod.

"You mean after classes and after you get your stitch fixed?" I asked with a teasing smirk.

She mumbled incoherently beneath her breath.

Frances had been created by Dr. Frankenstein, with some help from her parents, and on occasion one of the stitches holding her various body parts together came loose or snapped from being too rough.

She'd gone through a phase in elementary school where she'd had mismatched body parts. Everyone had teased her, and I'd punched a few kids who made her cry.

Her newest parts were top of the line, and she had even been able to choose them herself.

I had tried to convince her to get bigger boobs, but she refused. Not that she needed them. Her face was gorgeous and it was the only part that was completely her own, aside from her brain of course.

We moved forward at even slower than a snail's pace. I was pretty sure even a slime could have chased and digested us by now.

The night sky was full of stars and a half-full moon that gave off enough light for us to see across the field, but there were also special lights that let us see even more without taking away from the stars and moon.

"When's dinner?" Tsukiko asked.

Frances reached into her bag and pulled out a granola bar, handing it over to Tsukiko who immediately devoured it. Wolves had huge appetites that made them snack constantly. We'd learned to keep snacks on hand for our friend or she got a little testy.

"I think dinner is around midnight," I answered.

"That's so far away," she groaned around a mouthful of granola and chocolate chips.

We took another step forward.

"At this rate, we won't even make it to any of our classes," Frances said with a sigh.

"I'd be okay with that," I replied.

Looking around at the other students, I saw most grumbling to each other as well.

I started to turn around when I saw a handsome jawline and a prominent nose. Bogden. He was mostly human looking, except for his yellow eyes with a slit similar to a cat's. I tried to blame it on being a reaper, and having a love of cats who were half in and half out of this world, but it was more than that.

Bogden was kind and would stop to help another student pick up dropped papers, even if it meant he was late to his class and got in trouble.

He was also completely out of my league, and my dad hated immortals, so, just like my idiot friends, I was also crushing on an unobtainable man.

No, I wasn't crushing. I was just admiring. I could admire from afar. And I totally never thought about kissing him.

Almost never.

Rarely.

Not often.

Okay, daily.

"So, we've now confirmed that all three of us are hopeless?" Tsukiko asked with a knowing smirk.

I turned back around and lifted my nose. "I don't know what you're talking about. I'm just looking around. I'm allowed to look."

"Yeah, but that blush on your cheeks says you were doing more than looking," Frances said and poked my cheek.

I smacked her hand away. "Reapers do not blush."

Both of my friends rolled their eyes at me.

"Jerks," I muttered.

"Just admit it," Frances said.

"Nope," I replied and crossed my arms.

"Okay, but he's about to come over here," Tsukiko said.

I spun, eyes wide, to find out she was a liar.

I hissed at her. "You're such a brat."

She doubled over in laughter, and Frances joined her.

I rolled my eyes. "Whatever."

Another step forward.

"Won't the doc be asleep?" I asked Frances.

She shook her head. "She rarely sleeps."

The doctor was so weird. It wasn't just that she was immortal, but that she was definitely insane. It made her a great evil scientist, but super kooky.

After what seemed like hours, we made it to the front and got our schedules.

We shuffled off to the side to compare our classes and the three of us looked up with wide smiles.

We were in all of the same classes together.

"I owe your dad a batch of my famous chocolate chip and stardust cookies," Frances said.

"Only if you make a batch for us, too," Tsukiko said immediately.

I nodded my agreement. Her cookies were the best.

We looked down at our watches, and Tsukiko said in a super chipper voice, "Dinner time!"

She skipped off in front of us, her tail high and ears perked.

"I'm pretty hungry, too," I admitted.

Frances nodded. "Yep. Same."

We jogged to catch up to Tsukiko, locked arms, and hurried to the cafeteria.

There was already a long line of students waiting to get food, which made Tsukiko whine and her tail droop.

"At least we are here ahead of all those other students who still have to get their schedules," I said to try to cheer her up.

"Yeah, I'm sure we will get the best food," Frances added.

"You think they'll have dessert?" I asked.

Frances shook her head with a smirk. "You're such a sugar addict."

"I'm not an addict. I can stop after one more cookie," I said and pouted.

"You're going to get fat if you don't stop eating all that sugar," Frances said.

I glared at her. "Just because you and Tsukiko don't gain weight no matter what you eat."

"Don't be mad at us," Tsukiko said, tossing one of her braids over her shoulder.

"Any idea what the meal options are like here?" I asked and looked around the room to try to see what those already eating had on their plates.

Tsukiko tilted her head as she raised her nose in the air and inhaled. "There are too many smells for me to differentiate. So, hopefully, that means there are several options."

With so many different species in one place, I assumed there would be lots of options, but that didn't necessarily mean that there were several options for those like me who ate more human-like food.

"Hey, what are you girls up to after classes?" Bogden asked behind me.

I tensed, my heart pounding fast in my chest, and a bit of my dark magic seeped out of my fingers before I shoved them in my pockets.

"We aren't sure yet," Frances said, glancing at me for a moment before smiling at Bogden. "Why?"

He walked around me so I could see him and said, "A few of us are planning on having a get together tonight." He looked around to make sure no adults were near. "Just some light fun, of course."

"Where?" Frances asked. "Maybe we can stop by."

Bogden held out a folded up piece of paper to me with a smile. "We'll start at five. I hope to see you there." He glanced at Frances and Tsukiko. "All three of you."

I swallowed and took the paper, basically snatching it from him so he wouldn't see the black smoke leaking from my hand. "Thanks," I breathed.

He smiled and walked away.

I slouched forward, my body feeling exhausted after having been tense for so long.

Tsukiko patted my back. "If it makes you feel better, you only looked slightly terrified when facing him."

I groaned softly and put my head in my hands. "Crap."

Frances took the note from my hand and read it. "You guys want to make an appearance?"

Tsukiko shrugged. "Why not? It should be fun."

I shrugged, too. "Sure."

Tsukiko smirked. "Don't act like you aren't dying to see as much of Bogden as you can."

"Oh, I want to see him as much as I can, but I don't want to see all the girls that will be hanging off of him tonight," I whispered.

Frances narrowed her eyes. "Yeah, I'm not sure I can control my anger."

"You'll have to," Tsukiko said. "Because we are going."

"Are you going to be able to suppress your jealousy when girls flirt with Rathik?" I asked and folded my arms across my chest.

She growled. "They won't." Her ears flattened to her head and her tail twitched behind her.

I arched a brow as she had just proven my point for me.

"Whatever, let's just get some food and worry about what club we're going to choose," Tsukiko snapped and spun away from us.

Frances and I smiled at each other.

Tonight was going to be very interesting.

THREE

Dinner was so good that I went back for thirds. First, I'd had meat and potatoes. Then, I'd had some weird slimy concoction that tasted amazing. Last, I had tried a meatloaf that was several types of meats mixed together. Whatever it was, it was delicious.

I patted my full belly as I followed my best friends towards our fifth period, Monsterology.

Monsterology was super frustrating because they required us to learn about each type of monster and their body parts. I really didn't see the point aside from learning where they were most vulnerable when attacking.

"I have no idea what I'm going to wear tonight," Frances complained.

Loralie and I locked gazes a moment and both rolled our eyes at the same time.

Frances had twice as many clothes as Loralie and I combined. She had an outfit in every color and could mix and match easily.

The academy was actually pretty large, and after a few more turns, I was completely lost.

"Where the heck are we going?" I asked, sniffed the air, and scowled. There was a lot of wet dirt or something around us.

"We are on the third sub level and our classroom is just around the corner here," Loralie said.

Sub level?

I stopped and my hair stood on end. "Below…ground?"

Loralie put her arm around my shoulders. "Girl, you knew that most of the school was below ground. Don't act shocked."

Honestly, I had forgotten.

"I don't like being underground," I growled softly as I resumed walking next to them.

"We know," Frances said and patted my back.

"When do we get our books?" I asked to try to distract myself.

"I think they said they would be delivered tomorrow evening before classes to our rooms," Frances answered.

"Any idea how heavy they're going to be this year?" Loralie asked.

I chuckled. "As long as they aren't half our body weight like in fourth grade, I don't care."

Frances laughed. "Come on, it was pretty funny watching you lug that huge bag around. Plus, you got super strong by the end of the year."

I growled. "I also almost fell down two hills and face planted like a dozen times."

"Oh, joy, the triple narcs are here," Norma, a vampire with a chip on her shoulder, hissed as we walked by her in the hallway.

I snarled at her.

Loralie hissed back. "What's wrong, Norma? Can't find a blood bag to suck on? Had to resort to the fake stuff already?"

"Oh, please. I'm not a loser like you three who can't even get a date to a school party and have to resort to going with each other," she scoffed.

"No, you just latch onto some unsuspecting victim who doesn't realize until it's too late how insane you are," Loralie snapped. "Filthy bloodsucker."

"You're just mad because you know you have no hopes of ever defeating me in a fight," Norma said and took a step closer to Loralie.

I stepped between them and let my canines down. "I'll gladly tear your throat out. Want to step outside?"

"Girls!" Mr. Sampson, the Monsterology teacher, snapped. "Fighting is not allowed."

I flipped my braids over my shoulder as I turned away from Norma, showing her my back. "Shame, I wanted to snap that twig neck of yours."

"Sooner or later, people are going to realize what puppets you are and that you shouldn't be allowed to join us. You're just narcs who report everything to your daddies and try to get everyone else in trouble," Norma growled.

"You're just a pathetically bitter jerk who can't see past her own jealousy," Frances said. "It's really sad, Norma."

We walked into the classroom and Loralie took a deep breath to calm herself as we found seats in the back of the room.

"Someday, she'll get what's coming to her," I whispered.

"Hopefully, it will be at our hands," Frances said.

Loralie and I nodded our agreement.

By the time classes ended, I was ready to tear apart a herd of basilisks.

"Hey," Antoine, a werewolf I often practiced fighting with, called from across the quad with one hand raised.

We all stopped and waited as he ran over to us.

"What's up?" I asked.

"Want to spar real quick?" He asked. "I've had a stressful day."

I smiled wide. "Yes, please. I was just thinking about taking on a herd of basilisks."

He chuckled. "If you do that, it will take you another week to get that stench out of your fur."

I scowled, recalling the last time we had fought a herd and had had that exact problem. Frances's arm had been so covered in goo that she'd opted to just get a completely new arm instead of trying to get the stench out. "Yeah, you're right."

"You've got ten minutes," Frances said. "Then we have to go run my errand."

Right, we had to go see the doc to get her stitch fixed.

Antoine lead the way and we followed, weaving around kids as we went to the fighting ring.

We passed by Rathik and a few other nagas, and his eyes tracked me.

I tried my best not to let him know I had seen him watching me.

As much as I wanted to try to have a relationship with him, it was basically impossible.

Not just because I had a hard time talking to him, but also because I was terrified of snakes.

There were a few other students in the fighting ring, but there was a large enough spot available for Antoine and I.

"Kick his butt!" Loralie cheered me.

"Go, Tsukiko!" Frances added with a fist in the air.

Antoine chuckled. "It always amuses me that they cheer like this is a real fight."

"No claws," I ordered him. "I don't want to worry about blood on my clothes or tears."

He nodded and raised his hands up to his face. "Ready?"

I put my own hands up in a defensive position, smiled wide,

and nodded once. "Ready."

He launched himself forward and the primal side of my brain kicked in, taking over my movements and pushing out all thoughts.

This feeling of freedom was addictive and there were some wolves who gave in and ended up permanently as wolves.

That was why I tended to avoid fights like this in my wolf form.

Antoine was an incredibly skilled fighter and I knew if he really tried, he could defeat me, but he held back for our sparring.

"Two minutes," Frances called out.

I tried to move faster, to take Antoine down by surprise, but he spun around me, locked his arms around my neck, and squeezed.

I growled, but raised my hand in surrender. He had defeated me, whether I liked admitting it or not.

Antoine chuckled and released me. "You're getting better, but you really have to work on not telegraphing your moves. I saw instantly when you decided to attack me."

I faced him and bowed. "Thank you for the match."

He bowed back. "Anytime."

Turning towards Frances and Loralie, my eyes widened when I saw Rathik a few rows behind them, his fists clenched at his sides as he looked down at Antoine and I. His eyes met mine a brief moment, and then he spun around and slithered off with his lower body in his snake form.

"What was that about?" Antoine asked me.

I shrugged. "No idea."

Only, I had a niggling feeling that Rathik had been getting closer and closer to me and I had to find a way to stop him. He and I could never be.

Never.

FOUR

Dr. Frankenstein lived a twenty-minute walk from the academy, but a five-minute drive. Since we weren't allowed to wander off without permission, I opted to call for a driver to take us to and from the doctor's place.

The skeleton driving us in the taxi didn't talk, which was perfectly fine with me. I preferred not having to socialize with strangers.

Tsukiko had seen something behind us after the sparring match with Antoine that had saddened her. By the time I had turned around, I hadn't seen anything or anyone, so I had no idea what she had seen and I knew she wasn't going to talk anytime soon, if her narrowed eyes and crossed arms were any indication, so I would just bide my time and ask her later.

Loralie dozed beside me, her eyes closed and a light mist of darkness surrounding her. It was a defensive magic that prevented anyone, aside from those with a magical key, from touching her while sleeping. If an enemy tried to touch her while she was asleep, or unconscious, the power would seep into the person, grab their soul, and pull it out. Then, it would wake Loralie and she would reap their soul fully, taking it be processed in the afterlife. She said there were occasions when the defensive magic didn't activate, but it was very rare. Her father had told us to try to keep her from becoming too tired because he believed if she was too tired that it wouldn't activate.

Loralie's grandfather gave Tsukiko and I the magical key, so we could wake our friend without worrying about dying. Since Loralie napped often and we had to wake her multiple times each day, it was a wise decision. I preferred my soul inside of my body, thank you very much.

The taxi stopped, and I nudged Loralie in the shoulder with my elbow. "Rise and shine, Dark Beauty."

She grumbled incoherently, wiped her mouth with the back of her hand, and then opened the door.

"Wait here," I ordered the skeleton. "We'll be out in less than twenty minutes."

His skull bobbed up and down in a nod. He put the car in park and then propped his feet up on the dashboard and put his bony hands behind his head.

Tsukiko followed me out of the taxi and shut the door behind us.

The three of us stood, side by side, looking up at the spooky gothic mansion that the doctor resided in. When she had created Grandfather, she had done it alone, but now, she had a few students, several minions, and a full staff for cleaning and cooking. Grandfather said the doctor would forget to eat for several days, until she fainted from lack of food, if she was left alone. Her staff ensured she had food placed nearby all of her workstations so she could grab it and eat it even when deep in thought about her latest experiment. Same with water to ensure she stayed hydrated.

"Is it just me, or does this place get spookier every year?" Tsukiko asked.

"I thought it would get less spooky as we got older, but it's the opposite," Loralie whispered.

"Come on, you big scaredy cats. We'll be in an out in no time," I said, looping arms with them and taking them up to the front door.

Before I could knock, it opened with a large groan and Terrance, a zombie butler, bowed to us. "Princesses," he greeted us in a deep voice.

"You need to get those hinges oiled," I said and swallowed hard. "That's super creepy."

"Mistress Frankenstein has requested that we leave it so she has a warning if any intruders get by us," Terrance said and shrugged. His shoulder hit the bottom of his ear and the ear fell off with a splat to the stone floor between us. He looked down at it with a scowl.

Most of her zombies were in top notch shape, and Terrance was one of her oldest creations. Why was he falling apart?

"Are you alright?" I asked.

He muttered something, bent, picked his ear up, and said, "Mistress Frankenstein is on floor two."

Loralie pulled me forward, past Terrance, and up the stairs to the left.

Tsukiko let out a big breath I hadn't realized she had been holding. "Oh, dark gods, he smelled worse than usual."

"Is he sick or something?" I asked softly.

Loralie shrugged. "I didn't know zombies could get sick."

"You think the doctor knows?" Tsukiko asked.

"The doctor knows all," a deep woman's voice said above us.

We tilted our heads back to look up to the next floor.

Dr. Frankenstein was tall, light-skinned, and had black hair that no matter how much she brushed it never lay down flat. She looked like she had been electrocuted all the time. She also almost always had goggles on, which made her eyes look larger than they were.

"You popped a stitch?" Dr. Frankenstein asked.

I nodded. "Yes, Doctor."

She sighed. "Everything is falling apart. Someone must have cursed me again."

Again?

"Was it just one?" she asked. "You might be growing out of your current body. Though, I thought this body would be mostly permanent from here on out. I suppose I'll have to start searching for appropriate parts. Would you like to be blue? I think I can make you blue this time. Or red? Red would look really neat. Or purple! If I can mix the blue and red—"

"I just popped one stitch. I don't think I need a new body, but I will let you know if things change," I answered quickly. If I let her go off on a tangent for too long, she would just decide things for me and before I knew it, I would be leaving with a completely different body.

She spun away from the railing. "Hurry up here and I'll fix it. I don't have much time."

She never had much time.

"Yes, Doctor," I said and tugged Tsukiko and Loralie up the stairs, two at a time.

We reached the spot the doctor had been, but she was no longer there. We followed the sound of crashing items into one of the doctor's surgical rooms. There were five metal beds, wall-to-ceiling cabinets filled with jars of various items, including everything from bits of creatures to medical herbs, and a wall of steel tools that included surgeons' tools and hacksaws.

The doctor stood before a cabinet, tossing things out that were crashing to the floor, which were immediately scooped up by two female zombies wearing scrubs and placed on a rolling tray.

"Sit. Sit," the doctor ordered me with a wave of her hand at an empty table behind her.

I sat on it and Loralie and Tsukiko stood on the far side of the room with their backs to the wall.

"You two need anything?" Dr. Frankenstein asked.

"No, ma'am," they both answered.

She turned and eyed them. "You both reek of sadness. You as well, Frances. Boys already?"

"Maybe," all three of us muttered.

She sighed. "If reproduction wasn't necessary for some of you monsters, I would tell you to ignore the males completely, but alas, for the generations to continue, reproduction is required. You could always have arranged marriages by your parents."

"No!" The three of us yelled.

She cackled and then snorted.

Loralie and Tsukiko looked at me, and the three of us sighed nervously. She may not have known it, but our grandparents had discussed arranged marriages earlier in the year with us.

It wasn't until our parents had argued for a few hours that they'd given up on the idea.

I personally didn't think it was over yet, that they would bring it up again, but I for sure wouldn't bring it up.

Dr. Frankenstein grabbed a few more things and then marched over to me. "Which stitch?"

I showed her the popped stitch and she scowled at it. "This...is strange."

If Dr. Frankenstein called something strange, it was time to be worried.

"What?" I asked, my pulse skyrocketing.

She poked me in several places, took some measurements, and made several hmm'ing sounds.

Tsukiko and Loralie walked closer.

"Is she going to be okay?" Tsukiko asked.

"Shush," Dr. Frankenstein ordered her.

Both clamped their lips closed.

Dr. Frankenstein moved around me a bit and then said, "Disrobe."

One of her zombie assistants brought me a sheet.

Despite bringing it to me, no one turned around or gave me privacy. I was used to it and honestly didn't care, so I quickly stripped to my underwear, took my bra off, and wrapped the sheet around my boobs to cover them and let the cotton cloth drape down over my lower body.

Dr. Frankenstein snapped her fingers. One of the zombies picked up a pad of paper and a pencil, and the doctor went about taking measurements and having the zombie nurse write them down. She then restitched the one that popped and said, "I'll call if there's anything. If you don't hear from me then that means you're fine."

"Yes, ma'am," I replied and got dressed.

We walked back to the taxi and got in it in silence. The skeleton drove us back to the academy, and we walked into our dorm rooms without a word to anyone we passed by.

I sat on my bed and looked at my friends. "Do you think something is wrong with me?"

Tsukiko and Loralie exchanged a look and then eyed me with matching worried expressions.

After a moment, Tsukiko said, "If it were serious, Dr. Frankenstein would have kept you there for observation. She's probably just trying to find a way to convince you to let her make some adjustments like she always does. If she doesn't call, then everything will be fine."

She smiled reassuringly, but it didn't quite reach her eyes.

If I looked at this unbiasedly, then I would agree with her. The doctor liked to convince people to let her use them as guinea pigs. She constantly tried to get Tsukiko and Loralie to let her do tests on them. And she was always trying to convince me to let her make changes to my body or improvements. I would just treat this like I always did. Like the doctor was just being weird.

Yeah, she was just weird.

FIVE

TSUKIKO

I suggested we stay in for the evening, but Frances and Loralie insisted we needed to go out to celebrate finishing our first day and to distract ourselves.

Frances spent an hour picking out our outfits. Then, Loralie spent half an hour doing our makeup. She forced us to swear oaths never to tell anyone that she liked doing makeup. Death's daughter enjoying doing makeup would be embarrassing, or so she thought.

I didn't often wear makeup, but Loralie enjoyed doing it, so I let her do mine on occasion. Tonight, was one of those occasions.

Finally ready, we headed out of our dorms and to the forest on the south side of the academy grounds.

It took us at least five minutes to reach the bonfire that the students were hanging out around.

Frances's eyes were super wide as she moved closer to the bonfire, but about thirty feet from it, she stopped and her body trembled.

"This is close enough," I said. "I'm starting to sweat beneath my fur." It wasn't actually a lie, but I knew she disliked fire as much as I disliked snakes.

Ainsley, a harpy with silver eyes and hair, skipped over to us with a wide smile. "Hey, guys!"

"Hey," we all greeted her.

"How was your break?" I asked.

While she wasn't a close friend, I enjoyed spending time with her on occasion. She was nice and fun and one of the most honest girls I had ever met. Plus, she got along with all three of us, so it was never awkward when she was around. She was often super cheerful and brought our moods up even during dire situations. She was like a little ray of sunshine.

"It was horrifically glorious," she crowed and flapped her wings a bit.

"Oh?" Frances asked with a smirk. "What did you do?"

"My parents took me to their nesting place and taught me how to take out distracted sailors," she said.

"You attacked humans?" Loralie asked, her mouth in an 'O' of surprise.

Ainsley preened. "Yes."

"Lucky," Loralie murmured.

"It was so much fun," she squealed. "Did you three do anything exciting?"

We looked at each other, and I bit my lip. "Not really."

She arched a brow. "Hiding secrets?"

"We just did a bunch of boring exercises that involved learning which greetings were proper and which creatures were most likely to want a war with humans. Did some training, too, but not really anything fun," Frances said and sighed. "Super boring."

"Well, maybe I can convince my parents to let you guys come next time," Ainsley said.

"Wishful thinking," I said. "There's no way my parents would let me go."

"I'm telling you, we need a foreign exchange program where we could go to another country to learn more about the humans there and the differences between the creatures in other countries," Loralie said.

"That would be amazing," I whispered wistfully.

It would never happen, though. Our families were much too protective for that.

Plus, there were things way out of our control that required us to stay close to our parents.

"So, who do you three have your eyes on this year?" Ainsley asked, moving closer to us. "I've been eyeing Antoine."

I smiled. "You and Antoine would be super cute together."

They really would. And, I knew that he had been eyeing her last year.

She sighed dramatically. "We so would."

"Go for it!" I encouraged her. "None of us have a thing for him."

"Dibs!" She yelled and flapped her wings quickly, stirring up dirt around her feet.

The four of us burst into a fit of laughter.

"I think I see him over there," Frances said and pointed behind Ainsley.

Ainsley turned and smiled. "I'm going to go say hi. Have fun tonight, girls."

We waved as she walked away and I sighed, watching her walk right up to Antoine and start chatting with him.

I admired her bravery. I couldn't walk up to someone like that. Crush or not.

"We need drinks," Loralie said. "Come on."

Frances and I followed her around the bonfire, keeping our distance from the flames for Frances's sake.

On the opposite side of the bonfire was a chest filled with ice and drinks. There were also some bottles of alcohol.

Loralie, of course, went straight to the alcohol and poured some in three plastic cups, and then added some juice to them to make the drinks taste better. She handed us our cups and then raised hers. "To a great year."

Frances and I smiled and raised our cups, too. "To a great year."

A fourth cup raised and tapped against ours. "To a great year," Dante said, smiling wide.

Frances's eyes widened, and she nearly dropped her cup, but managed to bring it close to her chest and almost hide her shakiness.

"Hi, Dante," I greeted him. "How was your first day of school?"

It was an agreement we had come up with as soon as we started liking boys. If one of us was too flustered to talk to the guy we liked, another one of us would talk to him, so he would stay nearby and we could hear him talk even if we weren't the one talking to him.

"It was alright. I hated standing so long in that stupid line for our schedule though. It wasted half the day," he said, looking at Frances as he answered.

"We were afraid we were going to miss dinner," she said softly.

"Same," he chuckled and ran his hand through his flame hair.

Frances swallowed hard and took an involuntary step back as her eyes focused on the flames.

"Love the new style," Loralie said. "How is it possible to make flames look messy?"

Dante smirked. "It actually takes me quite a while to style

my hair. Once I do it when I wake up, though, it will stay the rest of the day until I sleep on it."

"How do you keep from lighting the bed on fire?" Frances asked, her voice squeaking way more than usual.

"The fire only burns when I want it to," he said. "You can touch it, if you want." He took a step towards her, and her eyes widened so much I thought they were going to pop out of her head.

Loralie stepped between them. "Hey, Frances, isn't that Ainsley? We should go say hi."

Loralie pushed Frances away before Dante could say anything else.

Dante turned to me with a scowl. "Was it something I said?"

I fidgeted and shifted my feet. Should I tell him? She had a huge crush on him and I didn't think it was going to go away. Would she be mad?

"Frances...isn't a fan of fire," I whispered. "I'm sure you've heard how terrified her grandfather was of it?"

His eyes widened. "Really? She's scared of it, too?" He looked after her and his face fell. "That explains a lot."

"She tries," I whispered to him. "Don't give up on her. Just...don't try to get her to touch the flames, okay?"

I spun around and jogged to catch up to Frances and Loralie who had moved even farther away from the bonfire now.

Frances trembled slightly and chugged her drink.

"It's okay," Loralie assured her. "There's no fire here."

"I know. I know. I'm being ridiculous," Frances growled.

"No, you're not. We're all scared of things and it's okay. It's great that you can admit your fears," I said and patted her back.

"He must think I'm such a freak," she whispered, and her head dropped forward.

"I don't think he does, but if that is the case, then it is his loss. You're an amazing catch. Any guy would be lucky to have you," I said, and Loralie nodded.

"Maybe I should just let Dad and Mom set me up," Frances whispered.

"You know they'll probably try to make you a boyfriend," Loralie said and swallowed hard.

Frances scowled. "Oh, dark gods. I didn't even think about that. They totally would."

"Look, all hope is not lost. If his fire really doesn't burn you, then maybe he could help you get over your fear of it," I suggested.

Frances shuddered. "I don't know."

"I'm not saying try it now. I'm just saying it is a possibility. So, not all hope is lost, Frannie."

She glared at me. "Don't call me that where others can hear."

I raised my hands in surrender. "Sorry, it just slipped out."

"Come on, let's refill our cups and enjoy the rest of our night. Tomorrow we have our first real classes, and we all know it is going to suck," Loralie said.

We headed back to the drinks, and I saw Rathik out of the corner of my eye. He crooked his finger at me and backed up into the shadows of the forest behind him.

I swallowed hard and said, "I'll be right back. I need to find a secluded bush, if you get what I mean."

Frances waved me off and I jogged into the trees after Rathik, following his scent a hundred feet or more away from the party before I found him leaning against a tree with legs instead of his snake lower body.

"Hey," he greeted me with a smile.

"H-hi," I replied, my smile wavering. As long as he stayed back and didn't shift to his snake body, I would be okay.

He stepped closer. "I was hoping we could talk more in person now. We talked a bit by letter over the break."

"M-maybe." Why did I always stutter around him?

"Well, let's start small, okay?" he asked.

I nodded. "Small. Is good."

SIX

LORALIE

Tsukiko was hiding something. I'd felt it the day she came back from her family trip and as I watched her run off into the trees, I felt it even more.

"What's wrong?" Frances asked as she drank from her cup.

She seemed mostly back to herself, which was good. I really didn't want her freaking out about Dante when she didn't need to be. It seemed obvious to me that he was interested in her.

"I don't think she actually needed to go to the bathroom," I said.

Frances's eyes widened and she looked in the direction Tsukiko had run. "What is she actually doing?"

"We should find out," I said.

"We are not spying on our friend," Frances said and folded her arms over her chest.

"Spy is such a harsh word. I didn't say we would spy. I said we should find out—you know, check on her. Good friends check on their other friends," I argued.

"You think she's in trouble?" Frances asked.

"No, but she's been acting different since her trip," I whispered.

Frances's face fell. "Yeah."

Truthfully, we had all been acting a bit different since our summer family trips. I didn't want to tell them what had happened and it seemed they all felt the same. Being pushed by my father and grandfather to increase my power and learn new things was great. However, the number of souls I'd needed to ferry had taken a toll on me. If it hadn't been for the girls and I developing our secret joint power, I wasn't sure I would be nearly as cheerful. Being death was hard.

I wanted to ask them what had happened, to see if they had experienced similar things, harsh experiences that totally changed their outlook on life, but I didn't dare ask.

It was putting a strain on our friendships which had revolved around complete honesty before. We used to tell each other everything, down to weird bathroom talks, but now...now there was something each of us was hiding. I would have pressured them, but I didn't want to tell them what had happened with me, either.

"Are we just going to walk after her? She'll hear us, if she doesn't smell us first," Frances whispered.

"Shadow traveling," I said.

Frances groaned. "You know I hate traveling that way. It makes me dizzy."

"Stop whining. Let's go."

She groaned again, but set her hand on my shoulder and stepped closer to me. I let out streams of shadow until it began to cover us.

"What are you doing?" Bogden asked.

I yelped and spun around, the shadows disappearing instantly.

Frances arched a brow at me and then turned to smile at the witch behind us. "Hi, Bogden."

"Were you going to shadow walk back to the dorm rooms?"

he asked. His eyes sparkled in the firelight, and I found myself lost as I stared into them.

"Yes," Frances answered and sidestepped towards me, purposefully stepping on my foot. "That is exactly what we were doing."

"I can walk you back to the dorms so you don't have to expend your magic," he offered.

"We don't want to trouble you," I said quickly.

He smiled, and it was like a fallen angel showering me in warm radiance. "It's no trouble."

"Um, we need Tsukiko, and—" I rushed to try to find an excuse.

"I'm here," Tsukiko said as she jogged over to us. "What's going on?"

"Bogden has offered to escort us back to the dorms," Frances explained.

Tsukiko looked at me. "Oh, um, that's awfully nice of you."

"Come on," he said and turned towards the path that led back to the school.

I looked at Tsukiko and Frances, but they both just shrugged and followed Bogden.

With a pounding heart and dread filling me, I followed.

Bogden slowed so that he was walking beside us and the traitorous Frances moved to the other side of Tsukiko so Bogden could walk right beside me.

"So, were you girls able to get into the same classes?" He asked softly.

"Luckily, yes," I answered.

"Which class are you dreading the most?" He put his hands in his pockets as we walked, and I noticed that the movement allowed the moonlight to highlight his arm muscles.

"Um, I, uh, probably History. It's really boring," I answered, my cheeks warmed as I stumbled to answer.

He nodded. "History is pretty boring. What period do you have it? Maybe we can entertain each other if we're in the class together?"

I stared at him. Entertain each other?

"Third," Frances answered. "She probably doesn't have the schedule memorized like I do already. You know, I'm the nerdy one of the three of us."

"Nothing wrong with being nerdy," Bogden said and smiled wide.

Oh, hell puppies. Did he have to be so handsome and charming?

"What period do you have History?" I asked. I both wanted and did not want him to be in my class. I hated having such conflicting emotions.

We stopped at the entrance to the dorms. To the left was the girls, to the right the boys.

He leaned close to me and whispered in my ear, "You'll have to wait and find out tomorrow." With no time for me to respond, he straightened, said goodnight, and left.

"Oh, your face is super red," Tsukiko teased.

"Shut up," I whispered and pressed my hands to my cheeks.

"What did he say?" Frances asked.

"He told her she had to wait until tomorrow to find out," Tsukiko said.

I glared at her.

She shrugged. "Having good hearing isn't my fault." She tapped the tips of her wolf ears.

"Anyway, let's just get up to our room so we can sleep. I'm..." a yawn interrupted my words and since it got my point across, I didn't finish speaking.

We made the trek upstairs and after cleaning the makeup off our faces, we went to our separate rooms and crashed.

Tsukiko, Frances, and I trudged into homeroom, eyes barely open, and took the seats we had claimed the previous day in the back of the classroom.

Our homeroom teacher, a centaur who asked to be called Mr. C, was really only there to give us important updates and make sure we came to class.

When we'd stepped out of our dorm rooms, there had been a pile of our books waiting for us. They also provided a backpack, pencils, and a notebook.

Surprisingly, the books were lighter than I had expected.

"Did you guys hear someone got caught sneaking off the academy grounds?" A female naga three rows in front of us whispered to her neighbor.

Frances and I looked at Tsukiko.

She scowled at us. "It wasn't me."

"They said they were trying to sneak off to see the nearby humans," the girl continued.

The male werewolf beside her, Benjamin, said, "There aren't any humans nearby. The nearest human is at least a hundred miles away."

The naga shrugged. "That's what I heard."

"Why would anyone want to go see the humans?" Tsukiko whispered. "Gross."

"Maybe it was a vampire," I whispered, and Frances nodded.

Tsukiko shrugged. "I don't know."

"Where did you sneak off to?" I asked.

Her cheeks reddened, and my curiosity grew even more.

"I just used the bathroom," she muttered.

"Liar," I said in a sing-song voice.

She huffed. "I'll tell you later."

Frances and I locked eyes over her head. Knowing Tsukiko, she would try to make us forget. This time, we wouldn't let her. This time, I would pressure my cute, furry friend until she spilled her guts and told us everything.

"Here's your news for the day," Mr. C said. "You should all have received your bags, supplies, and books. If you didn't, go see the office staff. I am told to remind you that you are not allowed to leave campus unless you obtain prior approval. That should be obvious, though. Oh, and anyone caught with alcohol will be punished. So, best to stay clear of it. That is all for today."

So, they'd found out about our party? Not too surprising. I assumed we were under a lot closer surveillance than the other students realized. Or, that could be my paranoia from having an overprotective father.

"Oh," Mr. C said, regaining our attention. "One more thing. If you didn't choose a club yesterday you must do so today." He looked at me and my friends. "Especially, you three."

I bristled. What was that supposed to mean?

"Yes, sir," the three of us replied automatically.

Frances sighed. "Can we pick something easy?"

"Like what?" I asked, turning in my seat to face her.

"We could join the prom planning committee," Tsukiko offered.

My nose scrunched. "Prom planning?"

"It's easy and you know those prissier females will do most of the work because they're such control freaks. We'll just have to paint signs or something," she said.

"She isn't wrong," Frances finally whispered. "Plus, we won't have to do much work until the solstice. So, that's like two or so months of free time."

"As long as I don't have to dress up in pastel pinks, I'll go along with it," I muttered.

Tsukiko smiled. "Great!"

Frances chuckled. "You were planning to force us to join anyway, weren't you?"

Tsukiko nodded. "I've wanted to join for a while. I want to be part of it since it's something creatures remember the rest of their lives. My mom talks about it all the time."

I sighed, resigned to my fate. "Alright, Kiko, I'll join you."

Her tail wagged behind her. "You're the best friends a wolf could have."

I patted her on the head between her ears. "Yes, yes we are."

"Don't you forget it!" Frances said and lightly punched her shoulder.

"Dismissed," Mr. C called.

SEVEN

"Fine, I snuck off to talk to Rathik," I admitted, my ears drooped and my tail in my hands.

"You...talked to him?" Loralie asked.

I pet my tail. "I talked to him a bit over the break, by letter, and I can, on occasion, talk to him in person. He has to have legs, though, and preferably his scales covered by clothing or something. Nighttime is best because then I can't even see them."

"You've been hiding this from us. Why?" Frances asked. "We're happy for you!" She smiled wide and hugged me.

I growled softly. "It's not anything great. We're just friends. He doesn't like me like that."

"Are you sure?" Loralie asked. "Most guys won't go out of their way to make a girl comfortable like that if they didn't intend to spend a lot of time with her. And guys don't seem to want to spend time with girls unless they like them."

"That's not true. Antoine spends time with me," I argued.

"You're his alpha. That's different," Loralie said and rolled her eyes.

Okay, she had a point there.

"Well, anyway, that was my secret. Now, it's all out in the open. Okay? Are we good?" I asked.

Loralie and Frances hugged me from each side and I relaxed, dropping my hold on my tail.

"Of course we are good," Frances whispered.

"Forever," Loralie said.

"I'm sorry. I should have told you sooner, but I was embarrassed and I didn't want you to try to force us together. If it's going to happen, I want it to be natural," I whispered.

They both nodded.

"Got it," they said in unison.

For some reason, I didn't believe them.

Classes breezed by until dinner, and I skipped towards the cafeteria with a smile, excited to see what we were going to get to eat.

Loralie stomped behind me, still frustrated because Bogden had been in our History class and had passed her three notes. She read them and then had to cover her mouth to suppress a laugh.

The teacher yelled at her and Loralie had had to sit outside for the second half of class.

"He didn't mean to get you in trouble," Frances said to her.

"Well, I did get in trouble, and he snickered when I had to leave," she growled.

"Snickered?" I asked.

"Yeah, it's a word," she snapped.

"You've been reading human romance books again, haven't you? Those teen ones?" Frances accused.

Loralie's cheeks reddened. "Maybe."

"What was it this time?" I asked. "Vampire? Werewolf?"

"Reapers, actually," she mumbled.

I stopped and turned to face her. "Someone is writing love stories about reapers?"

She put her hands on her hips, narrowed her eyes, and gave me her best death glare. "What is so surprising about that? Are reapers not allowed to be loved?"

My tail wagged behind me despite my attempt to stop it. "I just didn't think the humans would romanticize your kind."

"They romanticize yours, and even zombies, so why not mine?" She asked defensively.

I resumed skipping towards the cafeteria.

"Zombies?" Frances asked. "Seriously?"

"What's wrong with loving zombies?" Doug, a zombie who had been a huge flirt towards Frances a year ago, asked.

"Again, humans, though? Are they romanticizing humans being with all these creatures?" Frances asked Loralie.

"Sometimes. Other times it's two of the creatures getting together. Or, some halfbreed getting with a purebred," Loralie explained.

"Maybe it isn't humans writing it," I said. "Maybe it's a creature who has access to humans."

Everyone gaped at me.

"That's a really good possibility," Loralie whispered.

"I didn't realize that was an option," Frances said. "Now, I kind of want to try my hand at it."

"Writing romance stories?" Doug asked.

Frances blushed. "Yeah."

"Can I read them if you do write them?" Doug asked.

We all stopped and looked at him.

"What?" He asked. "Boys aren't allowed to like romances? Everyone likes a good romance."

"Loralie has some she could recommend that have a lot of action and battles," I said.

"Really? Awesome!" Doug cheered. "I'll have to see if I can

find someone to get me the books, too. Unless you have a dealer?" He leaned closer. "Just tell me the cost and where to meet."

I threw a hand up to cover my mouth to stop the laugh because he was being completely serious.

"You think I could make some money selling them?" Loralie asked.

"I think you definitely could," I said with a nod.

"You two going to help me smuggle in the goods?" she asked, smiling wickedly.

Smuggle in human books? It sounded ridiculous, but it could end up being really lucrative.

"You have to give us a cut, too," I said seriously.

Loralie rolled her eyes. "Duh."

We finally made it to the cafeteria, and I hurried to get into line. Antoine waved at me from near the front and gestured me forward. I didn't want to cut everyone, but I was starving, so I ran up to him.

"You look like you're ready to eat a herd of Minotaurs," he said.

I rubbed my elongated fangs. "I'm so hungry. I forgot my snacks this morning."

"Really! Cutting?" Malaria, a gorgon whose snakes were hissing at me asked.

"Sorry, I'm really hungry," I apologized.

"Like we aren't hungry?" she snapped.

"Malaria, just let her be," Antoine said.

She put a hand on her hip. "Oh, you've got a thing for her."

"No," Antoine said. "We're friends."

"Friends... right..." she rolled her eyes.

I set my hand on Antoine's arm, sensing his anger and movement before I even saw it. "Just ignore her," I whispered.

He growled once and then turned around and moved

forward in the line. I followed him, ignoring her taunting whispers behind us. Food came first.

I piled my tray high with everything that looked or smelled delicious and then found an empty table and started eating. Frances and Loralie sat with me five minutes later, having had to stand in line at the back.

"You forgot snacks earlier, didn't you?" Frances asked.

I nodded, my mouth full so I didn't want to talk.

"You could have asked us," Loralie said.

I could have, but I didn't want to. I needed to be better prepared and stop relying on other people.

"You have some trouble with Malaria?" Loralie asked.

"Not much," I said after swallowing my bite.

Loralie looked over at the table Malaria sat at. "Really? Because she is glaring daggers at you."

Shrugging, I ignored them all and continued eating. So much good food.

When I was finally done, my stomach was full and happy.

"You should grab some snacks, too," Frances suggested.

I nodded and got back into line to snag some snacks. There weren't very many snack choices, so I just grabbed the items I could keep in my backpack that wouldn't make it gross or get coated in anything.

We walked out of the cafeteria and I ran right into Rathik, his arms wrapped around me and I looked down at his serpent tail and within two leaps was halfway across the quad. He smiled, but I could see the pinched corners of his eyes, betraying the pain I had caused by running away.

"Sorry," he said softly and went into the cafeteria.

"You okay?" Frances asked.

I swallowed past the huge lump in my throat and nodded.

I was fine, except I had hurt his feelings again. I hated hurting his feelings.

Was it possible to get over my fear of snakes?

Would being forced to be near them help or make it worse?

I wanted to get over it. I wanted to be able to be around him even when he was in his naga form.

I would find some way to cure myself.

Some way.

Tsukiko was quiet through our last two classes, but it wasn't sadness. There was a determined glint in her eyes that had me super curious.

She had jumped twice in quick succession to get away from Rathik. It was actually pretty dang impressive.

"What are we doing tonight?" I asked her.

Loralie tapped her pen against her cheek. "I need to make a list of books and see if I can find someone to buy them and deliver them discreetly to me."

"You're all-in on this plan, aren't you?" Tsukiko asked.

Loralie nodded. "This could fund our trip."

Our trip. The trip we had started planning when we were six where we would run away from our families and travel to another continent to meet some sexy single creatures overseas. We would make them fall madly in love with us and then we would return home, taking our rightful places as leaders, and the guys would show up to sweep us off our feet, proclaiming their undying love.

Yeah, okay, it was super farfetched and unlikely to happen,

but we liked to dream. And if we were going to dream, we were going to dream big.

Most humans thought monsters were evil and had no love, but it was quite the opposite. While we did enjoy the darker side of magic on occasion, we also enjoyed flowers, chocolates, and guys telling us we were pretty.

Not that a guy had ever told me I was pretty, but I was sure it would happen.

Eventually.

"What in the Underworld are you thinking about that has you blushing so bad?" Tsukiko asked.

"Uh, our trip," I admitted.

"It's going to be amazing," Loralie said. "We're going to break so many hearts."

I chuckled. "Sure we are."

"Tomorrow night we have a prom planning meeting," Tsukiko informed us.

I suppressed my groan, but Loralie didn't, letting it out and rolling her eyes for added dramatics.

Tsukiko ignored her. "We are going to vote on a theme."

A theme?

"Don't we always have the same theme?" I asked.

Loralie nodded. "Yeah, Dancing with the Devil. And Lucifer always comes and dances with anyone who asks."

Lucifer was one sexy fallen angel. His once white wings had turned black centuries ago, but his face was as handsome as ever.

"I wouldn't mind dancing with him," I said with a smirk.

Loralie smiled. "I don't think anyone interested in males would."

"What possible other theme is there?" I asked Tsukiko.

She picked up her History book and said, "Heaven and Hell."

Loralie, who had been mid-drink, coughed as she swallowed her drink wrong.

My mouth dropped open and I stared at her in disbelief. "You can't be serious?"

"Why not?" she asked, looking up at us. "Why can't we change it up? They have done the same theme for hundreds of years. I think it's time we do something different."

"Lucifer is not going to come to a Heaven-themed prom," Loralie said. "I don't even want to go to a Heaven-themed prom. We're Underworld creatures for the most part. We hate Heaven and those jerks that live up there."

"Okay, then why not an earth themed dance?" She suggested.

"That might go over better," I said, still shocked she had suggested a theme that involved Heaven at all.

"What would an earth theme have?" Loralie asked.

"Human trinkets? Flowers?" she said, but they sounded like questions instead of statements.

"So, frilly stuff?" Loralie grumbled.

Tsukiko sighed. "I don't know. I didn't really think you would react so negatively to a Heaven and Hell theme. It wouldn't be just Heaven themed."

"Kiko, we are Underworld creatures. We are shunned by not only humans, but all of the Heavenly realm. Why would you think we would want a Heaven theme?" I just couldn't understand her logic.

"Well, because we've never had one," she whispered.

"I think it might be best if we kept that one to yourself, okay?" I whispered.

She sighed and nodded. "Okay."

"Are we going together again?" I asked.

Loralie and Tsukiko looked at each other and then at me and both shrugged.

It was my turn to sigh. "I guess we'll just wait and see how the year goes. We have several months until the dance. If no one asks me, but you two get dates, I'll find someone to go with."

"We're not going to abandon you," Loralie said. "Rule number one."

"No one gets left behind," the three of us said simultaneously.

"So, who is ready for watching some creature television before bed?" Loralie asked.

Tsukiko and I raised our hands and then laughed and climbed onto Loralie's bed, sitting side by side.

If it had been up to us, we would have shared one room, but the school refused to let us share. They insisted we all needed rooms of our own for when we became overwhelmed or wanted time alone.

The only thing was that we never wanted time alone. If something was wrong, I wanted my girls with me to cry on their shoulders and to let them cry on my shoulder.

After a couple hours of comedy, we switched to the news and I gasped.

"Another creature village was destroyed by humans today," the reporter said, showing a village of nagas completely destroyed with fire and several bodies still lying around.

"The humans responsible have not been caught. The most troubling question we have is: how are they finding our villages? At this time, we do not have any answers, but we want to remind everyone not to panic. Reinforce your barriers and ask the high witches to create new ones if you want, but we are still safe."

"For how long?" I asked softly, my heart beating rapidly at the sight of all of the fire and the dead nagas.

How many had burned alive? How many children had been killed?

The reporter continued, "The investigators are working extra hours to track down any information they can find. If you see or hear anything, be sure to report it immediately. Stay safe, monsters."

Loralie turned off the television with a scowl. "There were no human bodies there. That means that if it was humans that attacked, they all got out alive. Or, they took their dead with them."

"They are known for taking their dead," I whispered, swallowing thickly.

"Yes, but how could humans defeat a nest of nagas like that?" Tsukiko asked. "That nest had at least thirty adults. Unless a few hundred humans attacked, they should have been able to defeat them. Plus, they should have been alerted by their magical barriers of intruders. Or patrols."

"Yeah, this sounds suspiciously improbable unless they had help," I whispered.

"Who would help humans?" Loralie asked, disgust evident in her tone and the sneer on her face.

"That is the question that needs answered," I whispered. "Sadly, we won't have any answers."

"Dad is totally going to add security tomorrow," Tsukiko whispered. "Just be prepared for it."

I nodded and whispered, "Honestly, I welcome it. Even though it means moving around for parties and things will be almost impossible, it will mean we are safe."

"And I'd rather be safe," Loralie whispered.

"It's time for bed," I said and stood, stretching my arms up over my head. "I'll see you girls in the morning."

We hugged each other and went to our separate rooms, but as I lay on my bed, I knew I wasn't the only one who couldn't get the burned village out of my mind. All of those creatures...dead. And for what? Why?

I hoped we would find out.

Sitting in the middle of our glamour class, I realized something.

I was a total lost cause.

Bogden sat on the opposite side of the classroom, chatting with a few of his zombie and tengu friends. I could have gone over and talked to him, but I had no idea what I would even say.

"You're not being very discreet," Frances whispered in my ear.

"Cat!" Ms. Felonias yelled. She was a tall, slim woman with dark, black hair that hung to her waist, feline ears, and a silky black tail that swayed behind her as she walked around the classroom.

With a wave of my hand, I changed the glamour over my body so that I appeared as a cat to anyone looking at me.

Everyone else in the class did, too. Everyone except Darla who had transformed into a goat instead.

Ms. Felonias walked over to Darla and glared down at her. "Are you insulting felines? Or are you just awful at glamour?"

Darla bleated pitifully.

With a wave of her hand, Ms. Felonias removed Darla's glamour. "Try again and this time, a cat. Not a goat."

Darla tried again and this time turned into a cow.

I suppressed my laugh by pretending to groom one of my paws.

Ms. Felonias gave me a glare and smacked Darla on top of the head with a closed hand fan I hadn't even seen her holding. "No! You will stay after class and practice until you understand what a cat is." She walked away muttering angrily in a different language and the occasional meow.

"Revert," Ms. Felonias ordered us and plopped down in her chair. "Can someone tell me why glamour is so important?"

"To help us hide from humans," a female satyr answered.

"Yes. I'm sure you've all seen the news of the horrific events happening. It is important that you keep your guard up and do not let the humans catch you. The wolf clan has provided us with additional guards, which I am very thankful for. You children are the most important for us to keep safe. You are our next rulers and if you do not survive...well...we do not survive. I want you to remember that what we teach you here may be boring or frustrating, but it is meant to provide you with a necessary skill for surviving out in the world." She closed her eyes and said, "Class dismissed."

We packed all our things up and hurried out of the room.

A tall chupacabra stood in the hallway, spit dripping down his open jowls as he stood in a terrifying mixture of wolf and human.

Tsukiko nodded once at him and he fell into step behind us.

"Your dad really went above and beyond overprotective this time," I whispered.

She sighed. "I know. I told him a chupacabra was overkill, but he refused to budge. I decided it wasn't worth arguing over and left it. If he tries to keep him as my guard for longer than a month, I'll fight back, but for now, I will let him protect me."

Fighting back meant she would have to fight and defeat the

chupacabra. Looking at the tall, muscular, male had me wondering if she could actually do it. Tsukiko was a really good fighter, but she wasn't as strong as her male counterparts. And, the chupacabras were known for being really bloodthirsty and to have high levels of stamina. It didn't seem like an even match. Definitely not one I could see her winning.

"You're doubting me right now, aren't you?" Tsukiko asked, her cheeks puffed out.

"What? No," I lied.

She huffed. "You haven't seen me truly fight in at least a year. I've improved and have some new tricks up my sleeve."

"Oh?" I asked. "What tricks?"

She shook her head. "I can't tell you. That's no fun. You'll see, like my opponent does, during my fight." She tilted her head towards the chupacabra and I picked up on her hint. She didn't want him overhearing how she planned to defeat him.

"Got it. I'll never doubt you again," I said with a serious nod.

Frances laughed.

"Good," Tsukiko said, completely serious.

I rolled my eyes.

We stopped at our next class, History, and I groaned. "Can't we skip this one?"

"No," the chupacabra growled.

I turned and gave him my best glare. "I wasn't being serious and don't order me around."

He snarled and suddenly my scythe was in my hand.

He took a step back, eyes wide.

"Loralie," Tsukiko growled.

I tossed the scythe back to its place in the in-between. "Sorry. That was a reaction. I'm sorry." I looked at the chupacabra who nodded his acceptance.

Tsukiko and Frances watched me as we walked inside.

"Since when can you do that?" Frances asked.

"Since this break," I whispered softly.

Frances opened her mouth to ask more questions, but our teacher, the grey-haired owl shifter we lovingly called Mr. Who, barked, "To your seats!"

I ran forward and took my seat beside Bogden who smiled at me.

Mr. Who started class, talking about the first human attack on Vlad Tempest's castle.

Bogden slid a folded up piece of paper from his desk to mine.

I glared at him and refused to take it, then faced Mr. Who again.

Bogden wrote something else and slid it again, bumping the piece of paper against my hand.

Mr. Who turned around, and I put my hand over the piece of paper so he wouldn't see it. The last thing I wanted was for him to read the note to the class.

When Mr. Who turned back to the board where he wrote down notes, I unfolded Bogden's note.

What do you get when you mix a cow and a goat?
Mr. Who & Ms. Felinas's child.

A laugh escaped my lips before I could stop it, and I quickly crumpled the note up in my hand as Mr. Who turned around.

He glared at me. "Already, Ms. Reaper? Outside with you. I'll not have you disturbing my class today."

I sighed, gathered my bag, and walked outside.

I sat in the hallway, against the wall of my classroom, and closed my eyes.

The chupacabra looked at me when I first walked out, but quickly focused on the people walking by, since he knew I was no threat to Tsukiko.

A few minutes later, just as I was dozing off, Bogden walked out of the classroom with his bag and sat beside me, so close our arms touched.

"Hey," he said.

"Hey," I replied.

"Sorry I keep getting you kicked out."

I rolled my eyes. "Yeah, well, what did you do to get sent out?"

"I made myself laugh," he said and leaned back, arms behind his head. He looked over at me and smiled. "I didn't want you to be alone again."

I looked pointedly at the Chupacabra. "Not really alone."

Bogden scowled. "He here for you?"

I shook my head. "Tsukiko."

He relaxed. "I see."

I relaxed beside him and closed my eyes, imagining what it could be like if we were a couple.

If we held hands while sitting together.

If he put his arm around me.

"You okay?" Bogden asked. "Your cheeks are a bit red."

I rubbed them and turned away from him, letting my hair fall over my face. "Yeah. I'm fine."

"So, what are you doing Saturday? I hear there is going to be a killer party," he whispered in my ear, his nose bumping against my hair as he spoke.

"I don't think I can make it," I whispered. "Guards and all."

He sighed. "Yeah, I was afraid of that." He leaned back.

"I'm sure there will be lots of people for you to hang out with," I added quickly. "You won't even notice I'm not there."

"Why isn't your dad sending guards for you?" He asked.

"I don't need guards," I whispered. "Plus, he knows I'll just try to ditch the guards every chance I can get. So, there really is no point to assigning someone to me."

Bogden laughed and I felt myself smile. I loved the way his laugh sounded.

We lapsed into silence and I closed my eyes, resting with a smile on my face with Bogden beside me, our arms touching and our breaths in sync.

If only every day could be like this.

TEN

Tsukiko skipped towards the club room, her tail high and ears perked.

I didn't really understand why she was so excited about preparing for prom, but if it made my friend happy, I'd help her.

Frances seemed quieter than usual, but I attributed that to Dr. Frankenstein's weird curse comment and the human attacks.

Tsukiko's chupacabra guard sauntered behind us, his gait slow and purposeful and his long and furry arms swinging beside him with his back slightly hunched.

I knew chupacabras loved human flesh, so it made sense that with a human threat, her dad sent one to guard her. They could smell a human ten miles away.

Honestly, if they weren't so difficult to control, they would make great guards for all creature villages.

We entered the classroom, and as I expected, it was full of the prissiest girls in the school.

Malaria gave Tsukiko a glare and whispered to the two gorgons beside her, no doubt talking crap about Tsukiko.

Had we been on break, I would have fought her right then

and there, but I had to limit my fighting during the school year. Dad would forgive me for a few scuffles, but more than that and he'd punish me. His punishments were nothing to stick your nose up at. One time, he'd made me pick up hell hound puppy poop for five hours straight.

Hell hounds were adorable, but their poop was toxic.

There were several groups of tables and chairs, and already the cliques were forming. Tsukiko found an empty one for us to sit at and despite all the strange or angry looks we were receiving, she continued smiling.

Her chupacabra waited until Tsukiko was seated and then went out into the hallway.

"Is he really necessary?" Malaria asked.

"No," Tsukiko said, "but have you ever tried telling an alpha no? It's better to just deal with his presence than try to fight my father." She shrugged. "I pick my battles well, and that battle isn't worth it."

"Alright," Ainsley said, clapping her hands together. Her wings were folded against her back, but today she was shoeless and had her talons on full display.

That wasn't common for her. Had something happened?

"You've all joined the prom planning committee. This club is going to focus on fundraising and then preparing for the prom. As you know, prom happens on Winter Solstice, so we only have a few months! Let's start with theme suggestions."

"We do the same theme every year," the gorgon beside Malaria with silver and black snakes for hair said.

"What if we did a human theme this year?" Tsukiko suggested.

"Human theme?" Malaria asked with a sneer. "We going to kill each other?"

"We could get human items and decorate with them. Make

it brighter than our prom usually is," Tsukiko continued, ignoring her.

Ainsley wrote it down on the white board behind her. "Okay. Any other suggestions?"

"I like the theme we always use," a female satyr I didn't know said.

Ainsley wrote that down on the board, too, and asked, "Any others?"

"What about a heaven and hell theme?" Rathik asked as he came into the room.

Frances's and my head whipped around to look at him and then back at each other.

Oh, this made so much more sense now! That little brat!

"Heaven!" At least five of those gathered shouted.

"Are you insane?" Malaria asked. "Lucifer would be so mad."

"No one wants to celebrate that crappy place," the satyr female said.

Ainsley wrote it down. "There are no wrong options when we're brainstorming. We will write down every suggestion and then we will vote anonymously. Thank you for coming, Rathik. Please take a seat."

Rathik smiled at her and then shifted his tail into legs and sat at our table, facing Tsukiko.

Tsukiko smiled at us and dipped her head.

"Alright, any others?" Ainsley asked.

When she finished writing everything down, she passed out pieces of paper for us to write our top three favorites on, in order, and she would tally them up.

I wrote my choices down and folded the paper in half before placing in the center of our table. The others wrote theirs down and piled them on top of mine.

Ainsley flitted about the room, using her wings to propel her faster, gathered all of the pages, and then went back up to the board and started writing hash marks for votes.

When she finished, we all sat in stunned silence. Our normal theme and the human theme were tied.

"Our next meeting is in one week," Ainsley said. "Your homework is to write up ideas for decorations and games for both of these themes. We'll compare and choose our favorite one from the ideas received next week."

Everyone started filing out, but I made my way up to Ainsley.

"Hey, is everything alright?" I asked softly.

She tilted her head to the side in a very birdlike gesture. "What do you mean?"

I pointed down at her talons.

She curled them a bit and said, "I've seen firsthand what humans can do to an unprepared creature. I know the likelihood of them getting onto our campus is very small, but I'd rather be prepared."

"I know we aren't super close friends, Ainsley, but if you ever want to talk, I'm here," I whispered.

She beamed. "Thanks, Loralie. I appreciate it."

"So, how did things go with Antoine?" I asked, waggling my eyebrows.

She chuckled. "We talked for a bit, but didn't really do more than that. I did convince him to meet me tonight to talk more."

"Get it, girl!" I cheered her.

She laughed and shook her head. "Get out of here, Loralie. Your friends are waiting."

I waved at her and jogged out of the room. Tsukiko and Rathik were talking a few feet away from Frances and the chupacabra.

"Everything okay?" Frances asked.

I nodded. "Yeah, I just wanted to check in with Ainsley."

Frances nodded at Tsukiko and Rathik. "He asked her to hang out tonight. She's trying to come up with an excuse that involves us."

I smirked. "I got this." I cupped my hands around my mouth and yelled, "We'll see you later, Tsukiko. Frances and I have plans."

Her mouth dropped open and she looked at Rathik before looking back at us.

I grabbed Frances's arm and pulled her down the hallway, waving to Tsukiko as we left.

Frances waited until we were out of the building before doubling over in laughter, clutching at her stomach. "You're so awful!"

I shrugged. "She'll thank me later."

"Hey, Frances," Dante said as he walked by with a really handsome thunderbird at his side.

"H-hi," she stammered.

The thunderbird met my eyes and winked.

I was too shocked to do anything aside from stare as they went by.

"Well, at least I'm not the only one who looked like an idiot just now," Frances whispered.

I grumbled at her. "I was just caught off guard. Who is that?"

"Foreign exchange student," Ainsley said behind me.

I spun around and my scythe was in my hand again, aimed at Ainsley's throat.

Her mouth parted in shock.

I quickly spun it away from her. "Ainsley! Do not sneak up on people like that!"

"I did not sneak up on you. You were just too enamored with the new guy to hear me," she said, her eyes still on the scythe.

I tossed it away into the in-between again and sighed. "Sorry."

"So, I wanted to ask for a favor," she said.

"Oh?" I asked and arched a brow.

"Turns out Antoine invited me to hang out with him and a few of his friends." She kicked the grass with one of her talons. "Would you guys come with me? I don't know for sure who is going to be there and I don't want to go alone."

"No problem," Frances said immediately. She would do almost anything for a friend, which was why I often had to stop her.

I shrugged. "We didn't have plans, so I'm fine with that."

Ainsley jumped up, her wings flapped a few times to keep her in the air, and she cheered. "You two are the bestest. Meet me in the game room at five a.m.?"

We nodded, and she hurried off.

"Guess we need to go eat and change now," Frances said.

I nodded. "Yep."

She looked after Ainsley. "You're right about her. She's different now and different even since the party. She seems...scared, but it's more than that."

"Maybe it's just the human attacks," I suggested and shrugged. "No idea, but let's try to help her out tonight so she can be distracted. Okay?"

Frances nodded and smiled wide. "Operation love is under way!"

I groaned. "Don't call it that!"

She laughed. "Don't act like you hate love! Your dad married a fertility goddess, remember?"

"Come on, time to go," I said to change the subject.

I did not want to talk about my step-mother. Not now. Not ever.

ELEVEN

TSUKIKO

I stared after my despicable friends who had just abandoned me with Rathik.

I was going to make them pay. So much payback was in store for my dear friends and they were woefully unprepared.

"We should grab some food and then we can talk and hangout," Rathik said.

I nodded and followed him to the cafeteria. There were a few other students eating already and some in line, too.

We got into line, and I decided my hands were really interesting.

"So, do you think they'll actually let us change the theme for prom?" He asked.

I shrugged and sighed. "I doubt it."

Most creatures were super set in their ways and hated allowing new ideas or events to take place. It was really frustrating.

"I hope they'll let us do something different, even if we keep the same theme," Rathik said.

"Me, too."

We both piled our trays high with food and then found an empty table to sit at.

In silence, that was mostly comfortable, we ate our food and then put our empty trays in the proper slots.

"So, what do you have planned for tonight?" I asked.

"A few friends wanted to get together, so I thought we could go meet up with them and hang out," he said.

Hangout with his friends? Where were Loralie and Frances? Did they have plans? Could I get them to meet us?

I walked beside Rathik to the game room where some games, like air hockey and football, were available for us to play. There were also several couches and a soda machine.

"I haven't actually been in here yet," I admitted.

There were several males in the room, and only a few females, but luckily, two of the females were Loralie and Frances.

"You two!" I growled.

They chuckled.

I stomped over to them with my hands on my hips. "You are both in so much trouble."

"Hey, Rathik," Loralie said, smiling behind me.

"Hey, girls," he replied.

"What are you two doing here?" I asked.

"We were invited to come," Frances said. Her eyes darted to Ainsley who was chatting with Antoine and another werewolf I didn't know.

"Oh, cool," I said, my fight leaving me.

"There's an empty foosball table," Rathik said. "You want to play?"

"Sure," I agreed, turning to smile at him.

"You two want to play?" Rathik asked Loralie and Frances.

"Only if we can play against you two," Loralie said as she stood.

"I think we can take them," Rathik said with a smile as he looked at me.

My smile brightened. "We totally can."

Frances stood. "Bring it."

We walked to the table, teasingly talking crap to each other the whole way and then I stood beside Rathik on our side of the table and my pulse skyrocketed. We were so close that our arms kept touching accidentally as we spun the foosball handles.

"You two are going down," Frances said and spun one of her handles.

I rolled my eyes. "We all know I'm the best when it comes to hand eye coordination."

"Enough talk. Let's play," Loralie barked and dropped the mini soccer ball into the slot that rolled it onto the foosball table and started the game.

I spun my handle, sending the figures on it in a fast spin that hit the ball and sent it across the table and towards the goal.

Loralie spun her handle, barely managing to hit the ball back in the opposite way to deflect my near goal.

Before I realized it, an hour had passed and Rathik and I had fallen into a partnership that required very few words and mostly movement and reaction. I hit the ball into the goal for the tenth time and threw my hands into the air.

"Woo! We win!" I yelled.

Rathik turned and held his hands up so I could smack mine against his. "Nice!" he cheered.

Frances groaned. "We were so close!"

"Not close enough," I teased.

"Are you thirsty?" Rathik asked.

I nodded.

"I'll get us some drinks and meet you back at the couches," he said and headed towards the vending machines.

I walked between the grumbling Loralie and Frances. "Thank you."

They bumped their shoulders into mine and we sat down together, but with me on the outside so Rathik could sit beside me.

"That was fun," Frances said. "I haven't played that game in a while."

Loralie nodded. "We need to get one for the mansions so we can play when we aren't at school."

I nodded my agreement.

Rathik sat down and handed me a bottle of water.

I took it and chugged it.

Just as I started to relax on the couch beside him, a deep howl that made even creatures run in terror sounded outside.

I leapt up, but Rathik grabbed my arm, stopping me.

"It's the chupacabra," I told him. "I have to go see what's wrong."

"Don't just run out into danger," he scolded me.

Loralie turned into mist and disappeared from the room.

With Rathik a step in front of us, Frances and I moved to the exit and peeked out.

The chupacabra who had been guarding me stood over a body with a growing pool of blood.

I inhaled and gasped.

Human.

"How did a human get this far onto the grounds?" Frances asked, her hand wrapped around my upper arm and squeezing almost painfully tight.

"Alpha coming," the chupacabra told me. "Stay inside."

Loralie reformed behind us. "There were three other humans, but the guards caught all of them before they could make it onto the campus. This one was the only one who got this far."

"How?" I asked. "How did it get so far?"

"Stealth technology," the chupacabra said. "Get inside, now."

Rathik pushed us back and closed the door.

"No one is leaving until we're given the clear," he said to the rest of the room.

"What happened?" Ainsley asked, she and the other students coming up towards us.

"Humans got on campus," Loralie said. "They've all been killed, but we have to wait until we're given permission to go to our rooms."

"Humans?" Ainsley asked, her face changing into mostly avian.

Antoine set his hand on her arm. "It's okay, Ainsley. I won't let a human get near you."

Rathik swallowed hard and took several steps away from the door, his eyes wide.

Had I not known the signs, I wouldn't have understood what was going on, but Frances had had the same problem when we were toddlers.

I reached out towards him, but suddenly his lower body turned into his serpent's tail and his eyes turned completely snakelike. I stumbled back from him. "Rathik?"

Loralie looked from me to Rathik and her eyes widened. "Hey, Rathik. It's alright. We're safe. The chupacabra got the human. There aren't anymore."

"Why didn't the chupacabra smell it?" He asked, his S's elongated now that his tongue was forked.

He was almost completely snake now, and I continued backing away from him, heading for the bathroom.

"We know as much as you do," Loralie said. Her eyes darted to me and then back to him. "You need to calm down, okay? You're scaring people."

He looked towards the spot I had been and then searched the room until he found me. As soon as he opened his mouth to speak to me, I ran into the bathroom and slammed the door closed, locking it quickly.

Slumped against the closed door, I slid to the ground, wrapped my arms around my legs, and tried to calm the hiccuping breaths now coming.

Snake. Snake. Snake.

Rathik was a snake.

Snake.

Snake.

Snake.

TWELVE

Rathik was freaking out. Tsukiko had locked herself in the bathroom and was probably hyperventilating. The other students were scared, but so far seemed stable, aside from Ainsley, but Antoine seemed to have her under control.

Frances met my eyes and then she walked over to the bathroom and knelt by the door, whispering through it.

"Rathik, can you change back to your other appearance?" I asked softly.

He slithered back and forth, pacing in front of the door. "I didn't mean to scare her."

"She knows that," I whispered. "We know that, too. It will help her if you could change back, though."

"Defensive," he whispered. "This is my defensive form."

"We're safe," I reminded him. "The guard protected us like he was supposed to."

"Should have smelled it. Why didn't I smell it? Was it because I wasn't in this form? Am I hindering myself by being in that form?" He asked the questions too fast for me to answer, but I was fairly certain he wasn't asking me anyway.

The door opened, and I had my scythe in hand while several of the students had magic primed or claws extended.

Tanjiro, Tsukiko's father and the alpha of all shifters, stepped inside with a deep scowl on his face. He wore a suit and looked, for all intents and purposes, human. "Where is she?" he asked me. He looked at Rathik and then at Frances squatted by the bathroom and figured it out for himself before I could answer.

"She's fine," I whispered and then quickly added, "Father."

He was handsome for a forty-year-old man, and he had always treated me incredibly well. He set his hand on my shoulder and said, "You can put your weapon away, Lorie. I am here now."

I nodded once and let my weapon disappear, trying not to let him see how relieved his presence made me.

"Fetch her, please. She will be angry if I do it," he whispered.

"Yes, sir," I whispered and hurried to the bathroom.

"She's embarrassed more than scared now," Frances whispered.

"Kiko, your father is here," I whispered through the door.

There was shuffling, the water ran for a minute, and then Tsukiko walked out, looking fearless and ready to take on an army. She walked to her father and bowed to him. "Father."

He was standing between her and Rathik, blocking her view of the naga who was still in snake form. "The chupacabra will take you to the house."

"The house?" Tsukiko asked, her eyes wide.

He nodded. "Just until we figure out how they got onto campus."

"My friends—"

"The three of you will go," he said and smiled warmly. "I know better than to try to separate my triplets."

Frances and I bowed to him. "Thank you, Father."

He patted us each on the head and shooed us outside.

The body and blood were gone and a new chupacabra waited for us. This one had black fur and was more muscular than the previous one.

"This way, Princesses," the chupacabra said in a surprisingly clear voice.

Reluctantly, we followed him to a waiting limousine and climbed inside.

Tsukiko glanced back towards the room, her sadness palpable.

"It's okay," I whispered and squeezed her hand.

She sniffed. "I made such a fool of myself."

"No, you didn't," Frances reassured her and squeezed her other hand.

"I might as well never talk to him again," she muttered and threw her head back with closed eyes. "It's probably for the best. It would never work."

I didn't argue with her because I wasn't sure she was wrong.

We rode in silence until we reached the mansion and then we headed to Tsukiko's room.

Since we spent so much time together, all of our rooms had three beds in them so we could stay the night together.

We also had several pairs of clothes stashed in each of the rooms which got updated as we grew and needed different sizes.

Sitting down on our beds, we all stared vacantly at the ground.

Humans. Humans had gotten onto the academy grounds and almost made it to the game room where we were.

How?

Was it just their stealth technology?

But the chupacabra should have been able to smell them.

They should have been able to smell them miles away from the school grounds.

But they had gotten past the barriers and onto campus without being detected.

That was terrifying.

"So, how long are we going to be on lockdown?" Frances asked.

I rolled my eyes. "Forever."

"The rest of our lives," Tsukiko muttered.

"You three are so dramatic," Sakura, Tsukiko's mother, said. She was a werewolf with silver fur and was just as beautiful in human form as in wolf form. She had silver hair, a very thin frame, and was as scary as a chupacabra.

"Ma'am," I said and dipped my head in a bow.

Frances bowed as well.

"Girls, stop bowing. I keep telling you to treat me like a mother," she chastised.

"Yes, ma'am," Frances and I said, our eyes still down.

She sighed. "So, now that you are cooped up here for at least a week, what would you like to do? Would you like to come with me on a trip?"

We all looked at each other and then her.

"Father will not allow us out," Tsukiko said.

Sakura spoke quickly in Japanese and although I couldn't understand the words, I could tell from her tone that she was chastising Tsukiko.

Tsukiko bowed her head and apologized.

"You will accompany me on an errand. There will be three werewolves and one chupacabra accompanying us. Now, pull up your panties and come with me."

I coughed to cover my laugh, but Sakura's eyes darted to me.

"I am glad I amuse you, Daughter," she said and smiled.

"Can we get some food?" I asked.

"We just ate," Frances said.

"I'm hungry, too," Tsukiko said.

"You are always hungry," Sakura grumbled.

We stared at her in silence.

She sighed loudly. "Yes, I will have food picked up on our way. Now, come along, Daughters. We will go on this errand and get food."

With quick steps, we followed her, being sure not to get more than a couple feet behind her. She did not like dawdlers and I did not want to get punished...again.

"Are you three afraid?" she asked as we climbed back into the limousine.

"A little," Frances admitted.

"Good. Fear keeps you on your toes," Sakura said with a nod. "But know that you will always be protected. In fact, I was informed that your grandparents will be coming in a few days to discuss the situation and come up with an answer."

I met eyes with my friends.

We had to be part of that meeting, whether our families knew it or not.

I would find a way for us to eavesdrop so we could find out what they knew. One way or another.

THIRTEEN

FRANCES

I had expected an errand with Sakura to be a shopping trip or something along those lines.

Instead, we were driven to a super fancy creature restaurant, one that we were incredibly underdressed for.

Sakura strode in like she owned the place, walked straight to a table of three women in gorgeous gowns, and she sat in one of the two empty seats available.

Since there weren't enough seats for the three of us, we stood behind Sakura.

Sakura smiled at the three older women, witches from what I could tell, and said, "Do you have the items?"

The women looked at each other nervously and then each pulled out small parchment wrapped packages and slid them across the table to Sakura.

Sakura took them, lifted them to her nose one at a time, and inhaled. Then, she slid three envelopes across the table to the women. She rose and said, "Thank you," before walking away.

We followed her, expecting to walk out of the restaurant, but instead walked to an empty table on the other side of the restaurant.

She sat and waved at the empty seats. "Sit, girls. We will eat here."

One of the chupacabras took the packages from her and walked out of the building.

Tsukiko opened her mouth, but Sakura shot her a glare that had Tsukiko snapping her mouth shut.

"Order whatever you would like," Sakura said, opening her own menu. "I recommend the fish."

Tsukiko and I opened our own menus. I couldn't decide on anything.

"Sakura, ma'am, would you choose for me?" I requested.

She beamed. "Certainly, Daughter. I would be delighted."

"Me as well, please," Loralie said.

"You, too?" Sakura asked Tsukiko.

Tsukiko closed her menu and nodded. "Please, Mother."

Sakura lifted her chin and as if summoned by the movement, a waiter appeared at her side.

The waiter was tall, thin, pale, and definitely a vampire.

She whispered into his ear, and he nodded several times before walking away.

"A surprise?" Tsukiko asked, smirking.

Sakura smiled. "I know how much you enjoy surprises."

We smiled and then all scowled at the same time as the surprise of the day came to mind.

That was a surprise I hoped we never dealt with again.

"You are safe, pups. No creature, especially no human, will ever lay a filthy hand on you," Sakura said. She growled softly and the hair on the back of my neck rose.

She may have married Tanjiro for love, but she was one scary alpha female werewolf.

"Do you—" Tsukiko started to ask, but Sakura put her finger to her lips.

"It is not public knowledge," Sakura whispered.

We nodded our understanding.

"Again, do not be scared. You will be protected," Sakura said.

"But what about the other students? They're still at the school, right?" Loralie asked.

"Yes, but we have sent an entire pack to patrol the perimeter and a dozen chupacabras as well. No human will get near them," she said.

"Then why can't we be there?" Tsukiko asked.

"Because your fathers are too protective," Sakura said. "I would have left you there, just with additional guards, if it had been up to me."

"Will we be allowed to go back soon?" I asked.

"No," Sakura said. "Not until we talk to your grandparents and Frances's parents."

"When will that be?" I asked softly. My parents were incredibly hard to get ahold of.

"We already sent word to them all. So, hopefully, in a couple of days," Sakura answered.

The waiter returned with several drinks and a few appetizers.

Loralie and Tsukiko tore into the appetizers like starved dogs, pun totally intended.

"You two just ate a few hours ago," I reminded them with a shake of my head.

"They are growing," Sakura said. "It is natural."

"They're going to get fat," I muttered. I knew I was just jealous, but my friends also knew I wasn't seriously degrading them for eating so much.

"I could do with some weight gain," Loralie said around a full mouth of breadsticks.

"Loralie," Sakura hissed. "Do not speak with a full mouth."

Loralie swallowed. "Sorry, Mother."

"Do we have another errand after this one?" Tsukiko asked, her eyes darting towards the table where Sakura had taken the unknown packages from the witches.

"Yes," Sakura replied and took a sip of her wine.

I took a drink of my water and looked around the restaurant. There were several different creatures eating, but we were definitely drawing most of the attention.

"Do you come here often?" I asked Sakura.

She shrugged one shoulder. "On occasion."

"How do you keep the humans from finding it?" I asked, looking towards the front door nervously.

"It is heavily glamoured. There is a witch on staff who reinforces it when necessary, but if she were gone, it would still be fine. Humans could walk in and they would see a full restaurant of humans. The host would then advise them it was full for a private event," Sakura explained.

"What if they come back a different night?" I asked.

"They don't," she said. "Once they've entered the building, it gives them the creeps and they won't return."

The waiter returned with our food and set each plate before us, before bowing and walking away.

Sakura had gotten me some type of pasta dish I had not seen before. It smelled good, though.

Tsukiko, Loralie, and I set our napkins on our laps and waited until Sakura took a bite of her food before we picked up our forks and started eating.

Loralie had a black dish that looked like it was moving, but her wide smile was not the reaction I expected.

Tsukiko had a huge rack of ribs that were smothered in sauce on her plate. She licked her lips and looked at her mother who sighed and nodded, giving her approval to eat with her hands despite it being a nice restaurant.

I picked up my fork and took a bite, barely suppressing my moan. It was full of cheesy and garlicky goodness!

For the next fifteen minutes, no one spoke as we ate our food, savoring each bite with happy smiles.

Sakura finished her food and sipped on her wine more, smiling as she watched us.

I wiped my mouth when I had finished and drank some water.

"Dessert?" Sakura asked once we were all finished.

Our heads bobbed in unison.

Sakura lifted a finger and the waiter appeared in a poof beside her. "Dessert menus please."

He set them down in front of us and waited.

Another server came and took our empty plates away.

I skimmed over it and said, "Lava cake, please."

"Sundae," Tsukiko ordered.

"Flan," Loralie ordered.

"Flan," Sakura ordered.

He bowed, took the menus, and walked back to the kitchen.

"Were your meals acceptable?" Sakura asked with a smirk.

"It was amazing," I said.

"Delicious," Tsukiko said.

"Phenomenal," Loralie said.

"I'm glad you three enjoyed the meals. How are the meals at the academy?" She asked.

"Pretty good," Tsukiko responded. "But not as good as this."

"Nothing is as good as this," I said.

"I will try to take you girls out to more places like this," Sakura said. "What would you like to do tomorrow?"

"Don't you have work?" Tsukiko asked softly.

Most of the time Sakura and Tanjiro had to deal with the shapeshifters and, more often than not, they were away from home.

"Due to the circumstances, and that it is nearly impossible to get all of us old folks together at one time, I will be staying home until things are decided," she said with a smile.

"Can we have a spa day?" I asked excitedly.

Tsukiko squealed softly while Loralie scowled.

"It has been several years since we last had one. I'm sure I can whip up some beauticians and such for tomorrow. Let me step outside and make some calls," she said and stood.

"Really?" Loralie asked us.

"Oh, shut up. You like them, too. Just tell them to paint your nails black," Tsukiko said.

"Who doesn't love a good massage?" I asked and squirmed as I thought about it.

One of the werewolves went outside with Sakura while the other guards stayed in the room with us, leaned against the wall with their hands clasped in front of them.

I wasn't sure I would ever get used to having guards nearby. I wasn't used to it yet and it had been at least a decade.

"Your desserts," the waiter said and set them on the table.

All other thoughts left my head as I picked up the new fork and eyed my beautiful chocolate cake.

Cake was life.

FOURTEEN

TSUKIKO

After picking up some more suspicious packages, we returned home and Mom disappeared to her office.

Frances and Loralie took turns showering and then we all climbed into our beds and slept.

My sleep was fitful, dreams of snakes and humans attacking plagued me.

The next morning, we sat at the huge table able to sit forty in the fancy dining room meant for when we had important guests over. There really was no reason for us to be in there, but we had started using it when we were toddlers because we wanted to feel important.

Dad had scolded us once and then had decided he didn't care if we used it. Some mornings, like today, he even joined us. "Can you pass the butter?" He asked from the opposite side of the table.

I gripped the butter dish and then slid it across the tabletop.

It slid right into his waiting hand.

He smiled. "Thank you."

Mom sighed loudly and shoved a piece of roll in her mouth. She knew there was no point in reprimanding us because we had been doing this for a decade and would continue doing it for at least a few more decades.

"What are your plans today, girls?" Dad asked as he buttered a roll.

"We are going to have a spa day," Mom answered for us.

He paused buttering. "I don't want—"

"Here, Tanjiro. Don't get your fur matted," she said and rolled her eyes.

Loralie snickered and coughed to try to cover it up.

"Good. Tonight, we should be meeting with everyone to decide on a course of action," Dad said.

That had me meeting his eyes. "Tonight?"

"You were able to get ahold of my parents?" Frances asked.

Dad nodded. "They were difficult to get ahold of. I had to use a seer, but we eventually got in touch with them."

"What time?" Loralie asked.

Dad shrugged. "When they arrive. You know how they are. We will probably eat dinner first, though. I expect you three dressed nicely and to join us."

"Yes, sir," all three of us responded.

He nodded once and took a big bite of his buttered roll.

"What are your plans, Father?" I asked and took a bite of the sausage on my plate. I had drenched it in syrup when neither of my parents had been looking.

"I have a few meetings with pack leaders and then I'll be home a bit before dinner," he replied.

"Can you pick up some refreshments?" Mother asked. "For the dinner."

He nodded. "Certainly."

"Uh, don't you usually have your staff do that?" Loralie asked.

She was right.

"We've recently decided to start doing things like this ourselves. To help keep us humble," Mother said.

I arched a brow at her because I could sense she was lying. What were they hiding?

It wasn't common for them to keep secrets from me. Was it because Frances and Loralie were here? Was there some coup going on within the shifter community?

If there was, I needed to know about it.

Mom gave me a look that had me keeping my mouth shut to save my questions for later.

Once we were done with our food, we headed to the large bathing and sauna area where we would have our spa day.

Dad had agreed to build the area in order to try to keep Mom and I safer. He knew if there was a facility on our grounds, staffed by creatures we could trust, we would be less likely to leave.

It totally worked.

Sure, there were times we went elsewhere, but ninety percent of the time we just used our own facilities. Mom had to call in the staff when we wanted to use them, since we didn't need to have someone here that often.

The staff was scheduled to arrive in around thirty minutes, so we changed into our massage clothes which was just a breast band and a pair of booty shorts.

Mother had the largest breasts among us and fiddled with her top a few times to get the position right. Loralie, Frances, and I tied ours tight, smooshing our smaller breasts against our chests.

"Pick out your colors," Mother ordered us, smiling down at her chest in satisfaction when she finally got her breast band tightened comfortably.

Frances and I hurried to the wall of nail polish and looked over the hundreds of options.

Loralie picked the blackest black there was and sat in a massaging chair to wait.

I took down one teal and one pink colored nail polishes and stared at them with conflicting emotions.

Frances took down a reddish orange that matched her hair with a nod.

"Which one?" I asked Mom.

She regarded them for a few moments, giving them serious consideration. "The pink. That is a good color on you."

I put the teal back and sat beside Loralie in one of the other massaging chairs.

I twirled my hair and asked, "Would Father tar and feather me if I dyed my hair?"

Mom turned from her phone to look at me. "What color?"

I held up the pink.

Her lips twitched. "I think we can get away with it as long as you leave some of your hair your natural color."

"Will it make her wolf's fur pink, too?" Frances asked.

Mom shook her head. "No."

Frances pouted. "Sad. A pink wolf would be super cute. I bet the guys would fall over themselves to get to you."

A pang of pain hit me. I had run from Rathik...again. This time I had hidden in a bathroom. I wasn't sure I could face him again.

He probably didn't want to see me, either.

I had to go back to school, but I was going to have to pretend Rathik didn't exist.

As if it was so easy to do.

"Why the sad face?" Mom asked.

I put on a fake smile and said, "Nothing. So, what's new in the world of shifters?"

She sighed. "You couldn't wait until we were alone?"

"Since when do you hide things from your daughters?" I asked, giving her a glare.

She glared a moment and then her eyes softened. "You're right." She turned to Frances and Loralie and bowed her head. "I am sorry."

"What's going on?" Loralie asked, worry making her eyes widen.

"Our world as we know it is over. We are at war," Mom said.

"War? With who?" Tsukiko asked, her throat bobbing as she swallowed hard.

"The werewolves have decided that they don't want to be under our control any longer, though they haven't officially declared war on us yet," Sakura said. "And the humans clearly are at war with us."

"How did the humans find out about us? I thought we were still mostly myths to them?" I asked.

"We aren't sure," Sakura said. "Most do still believe us myths, but there are more and more who are learning we are real."

"Are our spells less effective?" Frances asked. "Are they seeing through them easier somehow?"

Sakura sighed and rubbed her temples. "We really don't know. We've been trying to figure this all out for months."

"Do you think the werewolves are involved or is it just coincidental timing?" Tsukiko asked.

Sakura growled. "We also aren't sure about that. We've considered it a possibility, but if that is the case, we would have to wipe out all of the werewolves."

"There are hundreds of werewolves," I whispered.

"Thousands," Tsukiko corrected.

My eyes widened, and I looked at Sakura for confirmation.

She nodded. "They've been able to work their way into the human's world easier than most and have even formed relationships with the humans. There are now thousands of werewolves. They spread more easily since the child needs only a tenth of a percent of the blood to become a werewolf."

That was incredibly disturbing.

"Ladies," a deep voice called.

We turned towards the entrance to the massage rooms and I stared at the incredibly sexy demon there. He had thick black horns that curled behind his head and sharp as sin cheekbones.

"I wouldn't mind cutting my face up on those cheekbones," Frances whispered as she leaned closer to me.

I choked on a laugh and shoved her away from me.

"This way, please," he said.

Sakura sauntered past him, and he bowed as she passed.

As I passed him, he lifted his eyes and winked at me.

I felt my cheeks warm and turned so my hair fell over my face to hide my blush from him.

This room had six massage tables and ten massage chairs with foot basins for pedicures.

"Pedicures first," Sakura instructed us when we finally caught up to her. "Then massages."

We nodded our understanding and got into three of the available chairs.

Frances immediately turned on the massage options on her chair and stuck her feet into the warm water with a sigh.

I chuckled.

"Stressed?" Tsukiko asked her as she slid her feet into the water of her chair.

"A little," Frances said, her eyes closed.

Right. Why would any of us be stressed? Just because humans were attacking monsters and we were going to be fighting against each other as well.

Everything was great.

Four demonesses came in and started getting their rolling carts ready with all of their supplies for giving us pedicures.

The demonesses all wore black dresses and had their hair slicked back around their horns, almost hiding them.

"Do you do a lot of work in the human world?" I asked the demoness in front of me.

She tensed a moment before finally nodding. "Did you pick a color?" She asked.

I held out the nail polish, and she took it and set it on her cart. Then, she grabbed a bottle of wash and a pumice stone and started working on my calloused heels and the bottom of my feet.

I closed my eyes and relaxed as she went to work.

After our nails and massages, we all felt a bit more relaxed.

We sat around the living room floor on the fluffy carpet eating pizza and drinking sodas.

Tanjiro joined us a bit after we had started eating and sat down and shoved half of a piece of pizza in his mouth without speaking to us at all.

Frances, Tsukiko, and I all exchanged glances and then looked at Sakura who was staring at Tanjiro.

He finished his piece of pizza and lifted his eyes to us. His eyes widened when he noticed us all staring. "What?" he asked.

"That's what we want to know," Sakura said. "You came in looking like a zombie without even speaking to us."

"None of you were speaking either," he countered.

"Because we were stuffing our faces," Tsukiko said.

He rubbed a hand down his face. "Everyone is on their way here. I'm just dreading the arguing that will commence soon."

"Are we going to eat together?" I asked with a cringe. Joint family meals usually ended with someone thrown through a window and part of the house on fire.

"No," Sakura said. "You girls will take food up to your room so you don't have to deal with any of the drama of having all of us old people together in one room."

That was perfect. We could go to our room and then sneak down to spy on our families.

"Did you girls have a relaxing day?" Tanjiro asked.

We nodded.

He smiled. "Good. I'm sure we will be able to figure something out soon, so you can return to school."

Tsukiko tensed slightly before shoving pizza in her mouth and looking down at her lap.

We knew she was embarrassed about what had happened with Rathik, but there wasn't really anything Frances and I could say to make it better.

Knowing Rathik, he would talk to her when we got back and let her know that it was okay.

We finished our pizza and a few minutes later someone knocked on the front door.

"That's our cue," I whispered to Frances and Tsukiko.

They both nodded, stood, and we ran up to our room.

Once the door was shut, Tsukiko faced me and asked, "What's the plan?"

I smiled. "I'm going to shadow walk us to the room and we're going to eavesdrop."

"Won't they smell us?" Frances asked.

"They can't smell us while we are in the shadows," I reminded her.

"Oh, right. I always forget that," she said.

"You know they'll be down there for hours, right? Can you hold us in the shadows for hours?" Tsukiko asked.

I nodded. "I practiced it a lot over the summer."

"Seems like we all gained some new abilities over the summer," Frances said with a smirk.

"What did you gain?" I asked.

She shook her head, grinning wide. "Not telling. You'll have to find out when I use it."

I rolled my eyes. "Alright, keep your secrets. Anyways, I think we should wait at least an hour after they start, because we all know they're going to spend that first hour making small talk about the past year and nothing useful will be said then."

Both nodded.

"We'll have to leave fast once they're done. They'll come looking for us or call us down so they can talk after they've finished," Frances reminded me.

I nodded. "Yes, I've got it all planned out."

"I hope they come up with something good. Something that doesn't require us to have bodyguards stalking us around the school," Tsukiko muttered and dropped onto her bed with a sigh.

"Yeah," I agreed. "But knowing them, their answer will be to triple the guards and set traps around the school grounds. They'll successfully trap us at the school."

"Which means no more parties," Frances said with a pout.

"And every move we make will get reported to our parents, which means no alone time with boys," I said.

Tsukiko fidgeted with her shirt.

"Hey, you know Rathik understands your fear. You don't need to be embarrassed."

"You'd be embarrassed, too," she whispered.

"I would," I acknowledged with a nod. "But, I wouldn't let that stop me. I'd still go after him."

"Like you've gone after Bogden?" Tsukiko shot back with an arched brow.

I glared at her. "You know why I can't go after him."

She rolled her eyes. "Your parents would get over it."

"Are you forgetting his family?" I asked. "They'll kill me."

"Now you're being dramatic," Frances said. "They wouldn't kill you."

"I'm not taking my chances. Plus, he's immortal and-"

"Perfect for you," Frances said, interrupting me. "I swear, you're so stubborn and for no good reason. Just go on a date with him."

I folded my arms across my chest. "If I go on a date with him, you have to let me set you up with someone."

She narrowed her eyes. "You have someone in mind already?"

I smirked and shrugged.

"Hey, it's about time to go," Tsukiko said.

I looked at the clock, and my eyes widened. It was. Where had the time gone?

"Gather up, creatures. We're going on a trip," I said, smiling wickedly.

"Spy time!" Tsukiko cheered softly.

Spy time, indeed.

SIXTEEN

I would never get used to the spinning and swirling vortex of shadow travel. Loralie moved us from our bedroom down to the conference room where our families were gathered to discuss the current situation.

She found a somewhat large, shadowy spot on the wall nearest the table and the spinning thankfully stopped.

Frances and I held onto Loralie's arms and we all focused on the adults at the table.

Loralie's grandfather sat in his usual cloak, but had his hood down, exposing his skeletal head. He could transform to give himself a face, but said that the skeleton was his true form and he preferred it. Beside him was Loralie's father, his hood down, but with a human-looking appearance on—the one he wore most of the time. Loralie's mother was a petite demon with thick horns that curved up almost a full foot above her head. She was one of the most powerful demons, reporting directly to Lucifer himself. She sat between the two reapers, but despite being smaller in stature, her aura made her seem as large, if not larger, than the males.

Beside them sat Frances's parents, both monsters created by

Dr. Frankenstein. They had green skin, a side effect to Dr. Frankenstein using decaying body parts to create them. Frances was created with fresh parts originally, but she said she didn't mind the green skin, since it let her look like her parents.

Next to my parents sat my grandfather, his body more " than human, but his speech was perfect. I never understood how he did it.

Together, they were the leaders of the monsters, the most elite creatures in all of the world.

Grandfather sniffed loudly and turned in our direction, but then he looked back at Dad and said, "We should homeschool them."

Mom sighed. "No. The girls need to be out among their own kind. They need to experience the other races."

Grandfather harrumphed, but did not argue with her.

"We should triple security and assign two bodyguards to each of the girls," Frances's father said.

I almost rolled my eyes. So predictable.

"We need to figure out how they are getting into the school and other protected areas undetected. How they got by three chupacabras is bothering me more than anything else," Dad said.

Same.

"Their knowledge is too strong," Grandfather said. "There is someone on the inside feeding them intel."

"We suspect the same," Frances's dad said. "But we have no idea where to start looking or who it could be."

"Satan has been trying to do some probing," Loralie's mom said. "So far he is coming up with nothing and that is royally pissing him off. He doesn't like not knowing things."

Grandfather rolled his eyes. "Yes, we all know how pissy the dark angel gets when he's left out of things. I'm surprised he isn't here right now."

"I am here and that is all that is needed," Loralie's mom said with a shrug.

Grandfather narrowed his eyes. "You report everything to him?"

She smiled. "Do not get so worked up, friend. I know when to withhold things."

I rolled my eyes. Here we go. The fighting was about to start.

"That's enough of that," Mom said, snapping her fan open to cool herself and gain their attention at the same time. "I think we should call in reinforcements."

Dad groaned and dropped his head back against the chair. "No, not her. Anyone but her."

"She's our best defense against humans," Mom said calmly.

"She'll wreck everything," Grandfather snarled. "She is a menace and should not be allowed anywhere near the children."

"She knows when to behave," Loralie's mom said. "I think she is our best choice."

Who were they talking about? Who was "she"?

"I say we still increase security," Dad said.

"What news do you have about the werewolves?" Frances's dad asked.

Grandfather growled. "They are trying to fight us peacefully, trying to institute a democracy."

"They want a human democracy?" Frances's mom asked with wide eyes. "Are they morons? Have they not seen the turmoil that democracy is having?"

"They insist it is more equal," Grandfather said and the disgust in his voice told everyone in the room all they needed to know about his viewpoint on that.

"Then we should avoid assigning werewolves to the school," Loralie's dad said.

"What about the chupacabras? Are they siding with anyone yet?" Loralie's mom asked.

"Not that we can tell, though I am rather suspicious after the one almost let a human into the room where Kiko was," Dad said and growled softly.

"Do they truly possess the ability to mask their scent?" Loralie's dad asked. "That seems rather unlikely for the humans."

"Perhaps they are being assisted by magical means," Grandfather said. "It wouldn't be the first time that a human and creature worked together."

"If that is happening, we need to find out who it is as quickly as possible," Mom said and snapped her fan closed.

"I shall make the call to her and we should allow the children to return to school in a day or so, once we have the additional security ready," Loralie's mom said.

Without warning, Loralie returned us to the room. We fell onto the floor, panting and dizzy.

"Who were they talking about?" Frances asked between gasps.

"I don't know," I whispered.

"Me, neither," Loralie groaned.

Someone knocked on the door, but we were too tired to jump into position.

Mom opened the door and arched her brow when she found us on the floor. "I'm not going to ask. Your presences are requested downstairs."

"Yes, Mother," we all answered and stood on shaky legs, reaching out to each other to steady ourselves.

She sighed, shook her head, and walked away.

The three of our gazes locked, and we chuckled, but quickly covered our mouths to keep from laughing too loud.

"Busted," Frances whispered and shook her head.

"Yeah, but she won't tell anyone," I whispered. "She's cool like that."

We hurried downstairs and were hugged by each of the family members.

Grandfather pulled me aside and into the smaller living room. "I heard a rumor that you were with a naga."

I tensed. "There are nagas at school."

"I'm talking about over the summer," he growled. "Nagas are not trustworthy, Kiko. You know what they did to me and our family. Keep your eyes open and do not trust them."

The urge to tell him that he was ridiculous was very hard to resist. Rathik was not untrustworthy. He was one of the nicest and most trustworthy creatures I knew.

"Kiko," he growled.

I bowed. "Yes, Grandfather. I will remember your warning."

"Good. Also, if you are becoming interested in boys, I can recommend some very nice wolves."

I jerked upright. "I do not want to be match made."

He raised his clawed hand. "Easy. I did not say I would match you. Just that I could recommend them. I know how you and your parents feel about matchmaking."

"I appreciate your offer, but I'm okay for now," I whispered.

He sighed. "Very well. Stay alert while at school. I think you should keep your claws out. Just in case."

"I'll keep them out when I'm walking around, but they're frustrating when I'm brushing my hair or using paper because they tear things so easily."

He chuckled and patted me on the head. "You'll learn how to do things with them, but you do what is most comfortable for you." He placed a kiss on my head and we returned to the foyer where everyone else was chatting.

Mother looked at me and I gave her a small smile to let her know that everything was okay.

She returned to her conversation with Frances's father.

"Girls," Grandfather said loudly.

Everyone stopped talking and turned to face him.

"We have decided to allow you to return to school, but there will be additional security and we are calling in a human expert," he said.

"Bodyguards?" I asked, frowning.

He shook his head. "Not this time, but if things get worse, then yes. But, you will be allowed to go back to school tomorrow."

Frances, Loralie, and I cheered and rushed to hug him.

"Hey, we all agreed to this decision," Loralie's dad said. "We should get credit, too."

With a chuckle, we made the rounds, giving them all hugs.

Tomorrow, was going to be the start of my school year ignoring Rathik. I could do it.

I could totally do it.

And I would only cry a little.

We walked into the school and felt the tension that permeated the air. Something had happened while we were gone. I needed to find out what.

Bogden walked towards us and Loralie tensed, her stride faltering when she saw him.

He smiled and stopped right in front of her. "Hey, Loralie. I was wondering if you were going to be able to return."

She swallowed hard and said, "It took some convincing, but they let us out of our towers."

Bogden laughed, and Loralie's eyes fluttered a moment.

Oh, zombies, she had it bad for him.

And her response was cute and funny. I hadn't thought she'd had it in her to flirt like that.

"So, do you have plans tonight?" he asked her. "I was hoping we could—"

"Hey, Bogden!" Sampson, a tengu with bright red hair and a giant nose called. "Isn't that your house?"

Bogden's confused expression was amusing as he turned and asked, "Why would you think my house—"

Everyone stopped talking as a house with extremely long chicken legs walked towards the academy and stepped over the fence.

A woman with a bulbous nose stuck her head out of a window and yelled, "Bogden! You need to take out the trash!"

Bogden dropped his head and groaned. "What are they doing here?"

"Is that really your house?" I asked.

He sighed and pinched the bridge of his nose. "Yeah."

The house stopped walking once it reached an open area in front of the buildings, squatted, and then the legs plunged straight down into the ground until the house lay flat on the grass.

Bogden turned and stomped over to the porch.

The door flew open, and Bogden and the old woman started talking in a strange language. Their rapid conversation ended when her eyes glowed red and she grew taller, glaring down at him.

He sighed and nodded once, defeated.

She shrank back to her normal size, patted him on the cheek with a smile, and walked off the porch.

"Oh, maggots, that's her," Loralie whispered, her hands shaking.

"Who?" Tsukiko asked.

"Baba Yaga," Tsukiko's grandfather called as he ran through the front gates. He paused before her and dipped his head in a curt bow.

"Wolf," she said and dipped her head in return. "You had a barbecue without me. Why was I not invited?"

Barbecue?

"We did not have a barbecue," he said.

"Nonsense. I can smell the burned human flesh still," she said and sniffed a few times. "It's still rather fresh."

"No, we caught humans trespassing a few days ago and we burned their bodies. We did not consume them," he said with a sigh.

Her mouth dropped open. "You destroyed perfectly good human? You knew I could be here within hours, my oven ready! You've gotten rather rude in your old age." She harrumphed and folded her arms over her chest.

He growled. "I am not old, hag. You—"

She turned to face him fully, eyes red. "Careful, Wolf."

"Mother," Bogden snapped. "Stop antagonizing Mr. Okami."

She huffed and mumbled something I couldn't understand beneath her breath.

"Follow me and we will brief you on everything," Tsukiko's grandfather said, turning and loping towards the main building.

Baba Yaga followed, but then turned and said, "Bogden, take out the trash."

Bogden sighed, turned, and went into the house.

Loralie, Tsukiko, and I looked at each other.

"Well, that was...interesting," I whispered.

They both nodded.

"There you three are!" Ainsley yelled as she flew over to us, soaring in a close circle before landing on her talons between us. "My room, now."

"Tsukiko!" Her grandfather called. "To me, now."

"Sorry," she whispered to Ainsley. "I'll come find you later." She jogged off and we turned back to Ainsley.

Ainsley flapped her wings. "Come on."

We followed the insistent harpy as she wove between students, a serious expression on her face.

Once we were in her room, she slammed the door closed, and locked it.

"What's going on?" I asked softly.

She turned and said, "The new guy has been asking about Loralie since you guys left. I wanted to warn you now because several of the other females are irritated that he is asking about you."

"That's not why you're upset," Loralie said and folded her arms across her chest. "Out with it, Ainsley."

Ainsley sighed and then covered her eyes. "I...I laid an egg."

I blinked slowly. "Okay. That's pretty normal for harpies, isn't it?"

She blushed. "I wasn't supposed to lay one for a couple of years. I don't know what to do with it. It's larger than I thought it would be."

"I mean, can't you just throw it away?" Loralie asked.

Ainsley's eyes bulged. "I am not throwing away my egg, Loralie! How could you even suggest such a thing?"

Loralie raised her hands in surrender. "Sorry. Sorry."

"What do other harpies do with their eggs?" I asked.

She rubbed a hand down her face. "I don't know. Mom hadn't had the talk with me yet."

Oh, dark gods. I was not prepared for this. I was so unprepared that it wasn't even funny.

"Why don't we find someone we can ask?" I suggested.

"I don't want people knowing," she hissed. "If they find out I'm fertile now they..." she trailed off and I got a really bad feeling.

Loralie looked at me, and we shared a look of worry.

What had our little harpy gotten into over the summer?

"Let's go to the library," I suggested.

Loralie groaned softly, but stood and headed to the door. "That will be our best option for finding information discreetly."

"Thank you!" Ainsley yelled and threw her arms around my

neck and then Loralie's. "You guys are the best creature friends ever."

We moved down the hallway at a brisk pace, waving at people we knew.

"Did you hide it somewhere safe?" I asked softly.

Ainsley nodded. "No one will find it and it won't get broken. The shell is actually really strong."

Loralie pushed the library door open, and we filed inside.

I beelined straight for the card catalog, opened it to the H's and searched for books on harpies. Then, I searched for eggs, too.

I handed Ainsley the cards for harpies. "I'll find these while you get the harpy books. We can check them out then go back to your room to read them."

Ainsley bobbed her head quickly and flew up to the second floor, scanning the cards and numbers on the shelves.

"Give me one of those," Loralie said and then disappeared into the shadows.

As quickly as possible, we located the books and carried them to the checkout desk.

The librarian was an Astomi with large eyes, huge nostrils that took up half her face, and had coarse purple, oil slick-colored hair covering her body from her chin down to her toes. She didn't ever wear clothes because her hair covered everything. She pulled out the book card, stamped the date on the page in the book and the card, then slid them into her filing system. "Books checked out. Return them within one week," she said in a soft voice in my head that reminded me of tinkling bells.

We all three bowed to her and carried our books close to our chests to keep the covers and titles hidden.

"Hey," Dante said, smiling wide. He stopped several feet away from us, his hands in his pockets as he faced me. His flame hair was shorter than usual, slicked back and a lighter red than normal.

"Are you sick?" I blurted out and then bit my lower lip. Zombies. I hadn't meant to ask that out loud. He was just far enough away that I was able to talk to him without freaking out too much about his fire. With it dimmed like this, it was even easier, but it really made me worry.

He tilted his head to the side, his smile disappearing. "What?"

I raised a shaking hand to point at his hair. "You don't have much f-fire today." Dark gods, why was my voice trembling?

His smile returned, and it felt like my entire body warmed up. "No, I'm not sick. I just wanted to try out a new style. Do you like it?"

Now that I knew he wasn't sick, I gave his hair another look. Truthfully, he could do whatever he wanted and it would look good. He always looked good.

"I like it," I managed to whisper. "I don't think I've seen you with short hair. It suits you."

His smile grew and he took a step closer. "Thank you. I'm glad you like it." He took another step.

With his flames so short, it was easier to be close to him.

He took another step, and I swallowed hard. This was the closest we had been to each other. The closest I had ever been to him. If I reached out, I could touch his shirt with my fingers.

"Are you busy tonight?" he asked.

He took another step and the heat from his flames grew even stronger.

My breathing grew erratic, and I took a step back.

His smile wilted, and he took a step back as well.

"I, um—"

"We have plans tonight," Ainsley said and put her arm around my waist. "Sorry. I need her help with something."

He nodded. "I understand. Another time?"

I couldn't move. My eyes were focused on the bright flames dancing before my eyes atop his head.

Fire.

Fire bad.

EIGHTEEN

Frances calmed down within a few minutes, but her eyes betrayed the sadness she felt. She opened one of the egg books and began reading.

"Is she going to be okay?" Ainsley whispered.

I nodded. "Yeah."

She gave Frances another long look before opening one of her books and reading.

The book I had was dry, boring, and I had to keep shaking my head to keep from falling asleep. How anyone read these for fun boggled my mind.

Aside from basic harpy information, I didn't find anything useful in the book I had. Though, I skimmed a lot of the book, honestly. It was either that or I fell asleep.

"Anything?" I asked Ainsley and Frances.

Both shook their heads.

"Can't you ask your parents?" Frances asked Ainsley. "Or another harpy female that is here?"

"I don't know how they'll react if they find out that I laid an egg so early," she whispered, tears welling in her eyes. "I don't want to be labeled a freak."

"No one thinks you're a freak and no one will think that either. We all go through puberty at different ages," Frances said reassuringly.

"Really?" Ainsley asked, sniffling.

Frances hugged her. "Really."

After a long hug, Ainsley wiped her eyes and said, "I'll go find an older harpy to talk to. I think there's one on the janitorial staff. As long as they don't tell my parents, I should be fine. I just don't want them trying to play matchmaker with me already. I want to finish school first."

Frances and I gave her more hugs and then left to head to our rooms. Ainsley accompanied us for a bit since we were going in similar directions.

"Make sure you turn those books in," Frances said. "I don't want the librarian coming after us."

"I will," Ainsley said with a nod.

We got just out of the room when Baba Yaga appeared before us.

I bit back a scream, but Ainsley didn't.

Her piercing scream echoed in the hallway.

Baba Yaga folded her arms across her chest and scowled at Ainsley. "Rude."

Ainsley swallowed hard. "I'm sorry. You just appeared in front of me and startled me."

"I heard you have an egg," Baba Yaga said.

Ainsley's mouth dropped open. "W-what? I don't know what y-you're talking ab—"

"Save it," Baba Yaga said and waved her hand. "I just want the egg."

"What are you going to do with the egg?" I asked, my eyes narrowing slightly. This being loved eating humans. I could only imagine what she wanted with a harpy egg.

"To eat it, of course!" Baba Yaga said.

"You are not eating my egg!" Ainsley yelled. Her hands slapped over her mouth once the shout escaped.

Luckily, no one else was around.

"It is unfertilized, correct?" Baba Yaga asked.

Ainsley's feathers ruffled. "Duh."

"Then there is no reason you can't give it to me. You don't need it. It will just spoil and stink up the whole school," Baba Yaga said.

"I don't know," Ainsley whispered and looked at us.

I gave my best expression-less face. I was not going to help her decide the answer to this.

"Do you want your room to smell like farts? Just let me have it, and I'll even give you one boon," Baba Yaga said.

Frances grabbed Ainsley and pulled her away from Baba Yaga.

I followed them over.

"A boon with Baba Yaga is worth a lot. Like, more than you could ever hope for. She could make most of your wildest dreams come true," Frances whispered.

They both looked at me, and I held up my hands. "I'm not getting involved."

Ainsley cooed and looked up at the ceiling. "That is true."

I loved her cute little nervous coo. It reminded me of chickens Frances used to keep as pets.

Ainsley turned and held her hand out to Baba Yaga. "You may take my egg to do with it as you please in exchange for one boon that I may use at a later date of my choosing."

Baba Yaga smiled wide and shook Ainsley's outstretched hand. "Bargain agreed upon. Our shake confirms it and binds me by magic to uphold my end of the deal. Just call upon me when you want to use your boon."

A burst of blue magic knocked Frances and I onto our butts

and a tiny blue lightning bolt symbol appeared on both Ainsley and Baba Yaga's wrists.

Baba Yaga rubbed her hands together and licked her lips. "Now, take me to your egg."

"We're going to head out," I snapped too quickly as I stood.

Everyone looked at me, but Ainsley just nodded.

I grabbed Frances's arm and dragged her down the hallway and out of the building.

Our escape was immediately cut short by Bogden stepping in front of me. "Hey."

All thoughts stopped, and I blinked at him.

"Can I steal you for a minute?" he asked, grabbed my hand, and dragged me away.

I looked back at Frances, my eyes wide and my silent plea obvious, but the traitor just smiled and waved.

Bogden led me to his house, and I tried to slow him down, but he was much stronger than me.

"W-wait, where are you taking me?" I asked, a lump of fear clawing it's way up my throat.

He pushed open the door and yelled, "Mom! I brought someone to meet you."

Before I could turn to escape, the door slammed closed behind me on its own.

"Mom!" Bogden yelled again.

"Sh-she's with Ainsley," I whispered. "Why did you bring me here?"

I didn't want to die. I didn't want Baba Yaga to curse me or something.

Baba Yaga stepped out of the back room, wiping her hands on her apron. "Why are you yelling?" She asked him, but froze when she saw his hand holding mine. "Oy!" she yelled.

A second Baba Yaga stepped out of the room she had just come from, wiping her hands on her apron. "Yes?"

My mouth dropped. "Th-there's t-t-two?"

The door opened behind me and a third Baba Yaga stepped inside carrying a large white egg. "Sisters, I've brought dinner!"

I looked between the three and my heartbeat spiked. Three. There were three Baba Yagas.

"Mom, this is Loralie. Loralie, these are my mom," he said.

Why was he referring to them in singular?

"You're introducing a girl to us?" The second Baba Yaga asked, her eyes bright and her mouth a wide smile.

"I don't like her," the first one said.

"Death's daughter? That's who you want to date?" The third one, standing behind us still with Ainsley's egg, asked.

"You'll have to excuse them. They are the same person, but split into thirds by a nasty spell. They are one person, but not. It's confusing, I know, but you get used to it," Bogden whispered to me. He stepped back so that he stood behind me and set his hands on my shoulders. "Her name is Loralie. Be nice."

The three Baba Yagas gathered together, whispering while occasionally looking at me. Their glowers giving away that they weren't discussing anything nice about me.

Bogden pressed close against my back, his heat seeping into me.

This was the closest we had been...ever. It calmed and excited me at the same time and now my heart raced for a completely different reason.

The three women turned to face us. "We are agreeable to letting you date her. You are young and we realize the odds are externally stacked in our favor of you not staying together."

I bristled, not liking that they were only letting us date because they assumed we would fail.

But then I also wasn't sure how I felt about them letting us date when Bogden hadn't even asked me.

"I, um, I—"

Bogden rushed forward and hugged each of them. "You're the best mom ever."

"Are you staying for dinner?" the Baba Yaga with the egg asked.

"Yes," Bogden answered before I could.

"Set the table," the grumpy one ordered me before going back in the other room.

What had just happened?

NINETEEN

TSUKIKO

Twenty chupacabras, ten wolfmen, and four hell hounds walked through the front gates of the school.

I stood beside Grandfather to greet them.

Loralie stood behind me, practically vibrating with excitement.

I sighed and looked up at Grandfather. "How long are you going to make her wait?"

His lip twitched in what looked like a snarl, but I knew was him trying not to smile. "Until I've greeted all of them properly."

Glancing over my shoulder, I gave Loralie a stern look.

She folded her arms across her chest and looked up at the moon like she was bored.

Frances stood beside her, smiling and trying really hard not to laugh.

Hundreds of students lined the buildings' balconies behind us, eager to see the new creatures sent to guard us.

The thirty-four creatures came to a halt ten feet away, and as one, bowed.

"You were summoned here to protect these grounds and the

students within these grounds. Humans infiltrated once already. I expect that won't happen with you all here," Grandfather said and growled deeply.

The creatures barked their agreement.

"Takumi is in charge of you all. Takumi, if you need anything, contact me," Grandfather said, looking at a rather handsome and young wolfman. He had blonde hair and fur that was spiked out like he put gel in it and had three golden earrings in his left ear. He was the youngest wolfman to graduate from the academy and become a guard. He also loved to torment me whenever he was nearby. I wanted to tell Grandfather to send him away, but—and I would never admit this out loud to anyone—Takumi made me feel safe just by being here.

Takumi bowed again. "Yes, sir." He straightened and looked at me. "Are we providing a guard for Tsukiko?"

"No," Grandfather and I said at the same time.

Grandfather gave me a glare, and I snapped my mouth closed. My tail swished behind me, but I quickly wrapped it around my leg.

"Not at this time," Grandfather amended. "If the situation worsens before I am able to return and you believe she needs a guard, then assign one to her."

My mouth dropped open.

"Even if she tries to argue," Grandfather finished with fire in his eyes.

I closed my mouth and looked down at my shoes. Fine. I got it. I would just make sure that that did not happen.

Behind me, Loralie danced from foot to foot. "Grandfather?" she whispered.

I looked up and saw his lip twitch again. "You may go," he whispered.

Faster than I had ever seen her move, Loralie cleared the distance between us and the hell hounds.

The hounds surrounded her, rubbing their bodies on her and licking her face and hands.

She cooed at them while scratching their ears and rubbing the bellies of the ones who had lain down.

The ferocious, black dogs had red eyes that reminded me of the fires of the Underworld, fur that resembled shadows and mist, and razor sharp teeth that could tear through flesh and bone with ease.

And Loralie loved them. As Death's daughter, she was capable of controlling the hell hounds if needed, but she had such an affinity for them that they just did whatever she asked.

"How long will she do that?" Takumi asked.

"Give her at least thirty minutes," Grandfather said. "She hasn't seen hell hounds in several months. I'll leave it to you, Takumi. Take care of my girls...and the rest of the students."

He added that ending like he'd almost forgotten there were other kids here.

Takumi bowed. "I will."

After Grandfather left, Takumi straightened and looked down at me. "You may not want a bodyguard, but I'm going to be keeping my eye on you, little wolf. You smell like trouble."

My body heated as did my face. I flattened my ears against my head and swished my tail back and forth. "I am not trouble."

Takumi flicked one of my braids over my shoulder with his claw as he walked by and said, "We shall see, little wolf. We shall see."

Frances looked at me with wide eyes, but waited until he was a distance away before asking, "What was that?"

I shook my head, swallowing hard. "I don't know."

"Looked to me like he was flirting with you," Loralie said. She walked up to us, one hell hound on each side of her. "Isn't he a bit too old to consider dating? I mean, he's an awesome friend, but dating is different."

"He's only seventeen," I whispered. They also spent a lot of time with Takumi, but a lot of our time had been eating snacks and talking about all the things we liked.

"Uh oh. Tsukiko has a crush," Frances whispered with a smirk.

I slapped her arm and growled. "Shut up. I do not. He torments me constantly and is a complete jerk." He did, but only in front of others.

"Uh, huh. Sure thing," Loralie said with an identical smirk to Frances's.

I growled low and stalked away from them. "Whatever. No matter what I say you're going to think what you want."

Ahead of me, Rathik stepped out of the building and our eyes met. He opened his mouth, but before he could say anything, I turned towards the dorm rooms.

Takumi looked up from the conversation he was having with a chupacabra, his eyes moving from me to Rathik and back.

I shifted into my full wolf form, shredding my clothes in the process, and ran off into the forest instead of going to my room. I didn't want to talk to anyone. I needed some time to myself to think.

Surprisingly, Frances and Loralie did not call after me or try to catch me.

Good.

With a burst of speed, I darted into the dark woods, weaving through the trees on silent paws.

Freedom.

This was absolute freedom.

In the woods, no one cared what my grades were, what I wore, or how I reacted to serpents. Here, I was free to be me.

I could hunt. I could sleep. I could do as I pleased.

Absolute bliss.

And yet...

Just at the edge of my range of hearing, I caught snippets of laughter and conversation.

Here I was free, but I was also alone.

As the daughter of an elite, I could not do as I pleased all the time. I would be expected to marry and produce heirs. I would be expected to rule over the packs with an iron claw. I would be expected to do so much.

I would enjoy my freedom while I could.

TWENTY

LORALIE

Tsukiko was off being a wolf and Frances left to study for a test we had coming up.

That left me alone with the two hell hounds I had adopted as mine. Takumi had been irritated, but ultimately, he gave up and let me take the two pups. They were very young, and I wasn't sure why they had been allowed out of the Underworld to begin with.

I didn't like the idea of them out on patrol when humans were sneaking past chupacabras.

The two hell hounds lay curled up at my feet, snoring. Tendrils of black smoke seeped from their noses as they snored.

They were the most adorable things ever.

I looked up at the ceiling as I remembered my dinner with Bogden and his mother. There hadn't been much talking, which had suited me fine.

I had only eaten the salad because the only other thing to eat was scrambled harpy egg. There was no way I was going to eat Ainsley's egg.

After helping with the dishes, I had excused myself and left without talking to Bogden.

I was still so confused about the whole event.

Why had he acted like he was getting their permission to date me when he hadn't even asked if I wanted to date him?

I mean, he was amazing and I was sure dating him would be phenomenal, but...it just wouldn't work.

Someone knocked on my door and the hell hounds were instantly up and growling.

I held my palm out and they both obediently sat down. Once I was sure they would stay, I opened the door.

"Hey," Bogden said, smiling and rubbing the back of his neck.

"Uh, hi," I whispered. "What's up?"

"You ran off before I could really talk to you after dinner," he said. "Are you okay?"

"Fine," I whispered, my eyes dropped to his chest so I could avoid looking at his face.

"Are you mad at me?" He whispered and took a step closer.

I jerked my head up and asked, "Why would I be mad at you?"

"Because I asked my mom about dating you without talking to you first," he said.

"Why did you? You never even said you wanted to date me or anything. Was it just to irk them?" I asked.

He frowned. "Come on, you know I'm not like that, Lor."

"You have to know this won't work," I whispered, looking down the hallway to see if anyone else was nearby. The last thing I needed was my parents to find out that a boy was at my room.

"What? Why not? We're great together," he whispered and took another step closer.

Suddenly, Takumi appeared between us, pushing Bogden back. "No boys allowed in the girls' rooms."

"Takumi," I gasped.

"Who are you?" Bogden snapped, his hands glowing slightly.

"Are you alright, LiLi?" Takumi asked softly.

"Takumi, nothing was going to happen. We were just talking. Why are you here?" I snapped, my anger growing.

The hell hounds stood, growling from sensing my anger.

"I'm patrolling the grounds, and I came to check on you," Takumi whispered. "It seems I had good timing."

"Loralie, who is he?" Bogden asked.

"He's just a friend of the family," I answered. "And he is leaving. Now."

Takumi stared at me a long moment and then bowed. "As you wish, Princess." He straightened and glared at Bogden. "Do not try to enter her room or the hell hounds will attack you."

The hell hounds growled their agreement.

With a smirk in my direction that Bogden couldn't see, Takumi bounded off down the hallway on all fours.

Stupid wolfman.

Though, he had just saved me.

"Look, Bogden, I really like you. You're great and handsome and everything most girls want, but a relationship between the two of us is just not possible," I said, gripping my doorknob.

"Does this have to do with him?" he asked, glaring down the hallway.

I laughed. "Not at all. He just wanted to upset you. Takumi's heart belongs to another."

I would never rat him out, though.

"Then why—"

"I'm sorry. It's just not possible," I whispered. "Thank you for dinner and for introducing me to your mom. Good night."

I shut the door right in his face, locked it, and then threw myself onto the bed, face first.

This was for the best. It was for the best.

It was to protect him.

No, it was to protect me...and my secret.

"Today, we will learn the proper way to cook humans," Baba Yaga said.

"No!" Takumi said from the back of the room and sighed, rubbing his hand down his face. "Not humans, Baba Yaga."

She sighed. "Fine, pigs. It's pigs." She turned and mumbled, "Should be humans. I mean pigs are close to humans anyway." She'd demanded she be allowed to teach us some cooking classes in return for protecting us.

No one objected.

"Your mom is crazy awesome," Rathik whispered to Bogden. Bogden, Rathik, and Dante were sharing a cooking station just behind Loralie, Tsukiko, and I.

We were well aware that it had been done on purpose, but we just kept facing forward, to ignore them.

Loralie wouldn't tell me what had happened, but she and Bogden had obviously had a fight of some sort. He kept looking at her like a lost puppy and she kept blushing and looking away from him.

Tsukiko trembled any time Rathik spoke. Her hands were in

fists atop the table and her jaw was clenched. She wasn't even speaking to him from what I had seen.

Not that I was much better. Dante's flame hair was low and slicked back, but I still couldn't look at him. We had gotten so close and then I'd frozen again. I was such an idiot. If Ainsley hadn't saved me, I don't know what stupid thing would have come out of my mouth.

"In the refrigerators at each of your stations is a slab of meat. I will put the recipe with instructions on the board and you will be expected to follow them. This is like a spell; you must follow the recipe and instructions in order to get this right. You have one hour and fifteen minutes." Baba Yaga tapped a claw against the whiteboard and the recipe and instructions appeared. "Begin."

"I'll measure the spices," I offered.

"I'll handle the meat," Tsukiko whispered.

"I'll handle the oven," Loralie said.

We all knew I wouldn't be handling the oven.

Taking my time, I carefully measured out each of the spices, putting them in the little dishes, and then began combining the ones that I could.

Tsukiko took the combined spices and rubbed them on the meat while Loralie preheated the oven.

I kept my eyes on the meat, not wanting to give in to the temptation to look at the table behind us.

Why were they torturing us? Was it to be cruel?

"Tonight, let's go hang out in the game room," Dante said.

My body tensed at his voice, but I didn't turn.

"I'm up for some games," Bogden said. "I know I could use a distraction right now."

Games. Was that what this was to them? Games to see how much pain and discomfort they could cause us?

One of their plastic spice containers rolled off the front of their station and towards us.

All three of us froze.

"Whoops," Rathik said.

Out of the corner of my eye, I saw him walking around his station to come retrieve it. It had landed right behind Tsukiko.

Suddenly, Takumi was there and picked up the container before Rathik could make it all the way around the station. He set their container on their station and said, "Here you go, friend." Takumi stood right behind Tsukiko, their backs almost touching. "You shouldn't let those get away from you or you might make a huge mess on the floor."

"Thanks," Rathik muttered.

Tsukiko reached a hand back and touched just the tip of her finger to Takumi's palm. A gesture of thanks.

I wanted to do the same, but I could already feel the anger seething from the three boys.

Takumi walked away, making a circuit around the room to check on the other students.

"How many favors do we owe him now?" I asked Tsukiko in a whisper.

She shook her head. "Too many."

Dante and Bogden also tried to accidentally drop something to get close to us and each time, Takumi came to our rescue.

By now, more than just our two groups were aware of the situation. I knew it wouldn't be long before some stupid rumor was spread.

We finished our pig and it came out smelling delicious.

Baba Yaga came over, gave Loralie a glare, and gave us a B with no reason as to why we didn't get an A.

None of us wanted to argue with her, though. We just accepted our grade and hurried out of the class.

"That was awful," Tsukiko whispered.

"I'm more tense now than at family gatherings," Loralie grumbled and shook out her hands.

"Hey," Ainsley called from behind us.

We turned around and waited as she jogged up to us.

"What's up?" I asked.

She flapped her wings. "What is the deal with you three and that wolfman? Are you guys sharing him or something?"

Had I been drinking water, I would have spit it out.

"What?" I gasped. "Ainsley, you should know us better than that."

"You all seemed pretty chummy with him, and he kept interrupting the trio behind you whenever they were trying to get close to you," she said. "Is he an ex and super jealous?"

"No!" All three of us yelled at the same time.

"He's a family friend. He's just super protective," Tsukiko said. "I refused to have a bodyguard assigned to me, so he's being a jerk and being overprotective to get back at me for it."

"He's just a family friend," I added again.

Ainsley pouted. "Well, that's boring. I guess I'll go straighten everyone out before the rumors get too crazy."

"Princesses," Takumi said from behind us.

We turned around, and he bowed to us.

This guy...

"What is it, Takumi?" Loralie asked.

"I finished my rounds and found nothing amiss," he said, standing straight and looking stoic.

Tsukiko scowled. "Okay? Why are you telling us?"

"As Princess, I thought it was proper for me to inform you," he said.

"We aren't princesses," Loralie snapped.

He dropped to one knee and bowed his head. "I apologize, Princess Loralie. I did not mean to upset you. I shall take my punishment as you see fit to give me."

Loralie looked at Tsukiko and I, her mouth opening and closing with no sound coming out.

"Stop being ridiculous," Tsukiko growled. "What game are you playing?"

"I live to serve you three," he said, still on one knee with one fist on the ground.

"Some family friend," Ainsley whispered behind me.

Satan, take me now.

"Stand up," Loralie hissed.

Takumi stood and smiled at her.

"Tsukiko," Rathik called as he, Bogden, and Dante headed towards us. All three wore matching scowls, and a dark red aura surrounded them.

Tsukiko tensed, and Loralie and I moved a step closer to her, the three of us touching arms.

Takumi's smile disappeared into a deep scowl. He spun around and took a large step away from us, blocking the trio from approaching. "They are not interested in speaking to you three."

"What is this?" Rathik asked Tsukiko.

"Come on," Tsukiko whispered and grabbed Loralie and my hands.

We turned and headed towards the dormitory, ready to hide out for the rest of the night.

"Frances," Dante called.

There was movement and then the sound of flesh hitting flesh.

"They do not wish to speak to you three. Do not make me say it again," Takumi growled.

I turned and stared in shock at Dante on his butt before Takumi who was more wolf than man at the moment, his fur dripping with black smoke.

"Takumi," I gasped. "Back off."

"Who is he to you?" Dante asked.

"I am theirs," Takumi said.

"No, you're not!" Loralie, Tsukiko, and I yelled at the same time.

"He's a family friend," Ainsley said from behind the boys. "Apparently, he's just pestering them because they don't want a bodyguard."

"Is that what you told her?" Takumi asked and looked back at us, pain flashing across his face for a brief moment.

"Stop this," Tsukiko growled and took a step closer to Takumi. "Why are you purposefully making people think we're more than friends?"

"We're not?" he asked, moving a step closer to her.

"Takumi," she groaned and let her head fall back.

"Did our time together over the summer mean so little?" he whispered.

"Apparently less than our time together," I whispered to Loralie who nodded.

We both already knew that he had a crush on Tsukiko. And all three of us had spent time with Takumi separately and together. He was commonly used by our parents to protect us, since we all actually liked him and could tolerate being protected by him.

"I swore my life to you three," he whispered.

"At different times," I said and put my hands on my hips. "You can't offer your life to multiple people."

"You three are one," he said nonchalantly.

Did he know about our secret ability? He couldn't possibly know. Yet, he was the only one who had made such a comment.

"You and I are not dating," Tsukiko said sternly. "Stop trying to make people believe that."

"Tsukiko," he whispered and stepped closer to her. "Were

you just playing with my heart this summer? Do you not remember...this..."

His face shifted and within a second, he had his human mouth pressed to hers.

Rathik hissed, but instead of trying to pull them apart, he spun and walked away.

Tsukiko pushed Takumi away and roared. "Stop this!"

Takumi shifted his head back, bowed, and ran off to the side of the dormitory building.

Dante stood and looked at me with a scowl, shook his head, and walked after Rathik.

Bogden looked at Loralie, their eyes meeting, and after a moment, he exhaled and went after his friends.

Tsukiko wiped her mouth with her sleeve and growled. "He's gone too far this time."

"Let's go," I whispered, noticing that we had gathered a crowd of onlookers.

Despite knowing that it was probably for the best and this would keep them away from us, my heart hurt.

I had never wanted to hurt Dante. And Takumi was only a friend, but...

It might prove to have been the best action.

TWENTY-TWO

TSUKIKO

He was ruining everything! Stupid Takumi!

No doubt the school was running wild with their versions of what they had witnessed.

Why? Why was he doing this?

Why had he kissed me?

My lips still tingled from his kiss, even hours later.

I growled and paced across my room.

How could I fix this?

I couldn't be with Rathik, but that didn't mean I wanted him to hate me. Or for him to think I was messing around with Takumi.

It was true that Takumi had pledged his life to us, but not romantically.

Keeping away from Takumi was my best bet, but he kept sneaking up on me.

Had Grandfather put him up to this? Or was this all Takumi's idea?

Loralie had tried to tell me that Takumi had feelings for me.

I hadn't believed her then, but now...she might have been right.

"Pacing and growling won't accomplish anything aside from making you even angrier," Frances said from where she lay on the ground, her arm over her eyes.

"I'm going for a run," I said and stomped towards the door.

"We'll be here," Loralie said from her spot on the bed, her face pressed into the pillows.

I shut the door behind me before shifting and running out to the forest.

A few other wolves yipped at me, but I wasn't in the mood to play. I wasn't in the mood to socialize.

I just wanted to run and hunt.

To tear something apart with my teeth.

I ran deeper and deeper into the forest, not caring how far from the school I was, or whether I ran outside of the boundaries or not.

A strange scent caught my nose and I turned, following it.

It was sweet and yet smelled of decay at the same time.

Slowing, I continued to follow the scent, but quieter and more stealthily.

As I turned for a third time, I finally found the source of the scent.

Two humans in strange suits and wearing weird helmets battled with Takumi.

Without thinking, I ran forward and tackled the one closest to me.

"Kiko!" Takumi yelled. "What are you doing here?"

I didn't answer, not that I could have in wolf form anyway, focused on trying to bite through the stupid suit the human wore.

The human grunted, my over three hundred pounds in wolf form crushing the wind from his lungs. His hand moved and then an electric shock went through me.

I yelped and jumped back.

The shock had been strong enough to blur my vision, and I shook my head to try to clear it.

Takumi tore the human he was fighting apart, his claws finally getting through the suit, and then raced towards me.

The human who had shocked me advanced, a strange metal strap in his hands. "Don't worry, we won't kill you," he crooned.

I shifted into wolfman form and said, "You won't do anything except die."

The human pulled something from his hip.

Takumi yelled my name, running between me and the human.

A loud explosion sounded, and then Takumi fell against me, the scent of his blood filling my nostrils.

"Takumi!" I yelled. I rolled him off me, pounced on the human, and tore at his suit with my claws. One of my claws caught and tore the material away, giving me a perfect spot to kill the human.

He cried out as he died, but I had no sympathy for him. I tossed his body away and rushed back to Takumi.

"Takumi, talk to me," I whispered as I knelt by him.

His breathing was ragged and shallow. "Princess, what were you doing out here?"

"I needed to go for a run and a strange scent drew me this way," I whispered.

There was so much blood everywhere. It soaked the ground below us.

"You came after me," he whispered and chuckled. His chuckle ended in a cough and blood dripped from his mouth.

"Don't you dare die on me," I growled. "You promised me your life, remember?"

He set his hand on my cheek, keeping his claws away from my skin. "I used my life to protect yours. That was what I wanted."

Tears blinded me. "I need to get you back to a doctor."

I picked him up, glad for my strength but still awkward at holding him since he was so much larger than me, and ran back towards the school.

"It's too late and you know it," he whispered.

"Shut up," I growled. "You'll be fine."

He kissed my cheek. "I love you, Kiko."

Wolfmen and chupacabras came into view, running towards us.

I was so close. So close.

"Takumi," I whispered, looking down at his face.

He gave me one last smile and then released a shuddering breath and stilled.

I set his body on the ground and screamed.

Loralie appeared out of the shadows beside me with Frances.

Loralie gasped and reached out, grabbing onto something above Takumi's body. "No! No! Takumi, no!" She sobbed, tears flowing down her face like they were mine.

Frances dropped to her knees beside me, looped an arm around my waist, and joined me in crying.

"It's too soon!" Loralie screamed, her hands clenching something so tight that her knuckles were white.

"It is his time," Death, Loralie's father said as he appeared behind her. He set a hand on her shoulder. "You must reap his soul."

Loralie shook her head. "Not him! Not Takumi!"

"Either I will do it, or you will," Death said.

Loralie sobbed and then disappeared in a flash of black light.

"She will return tomorrow," Death said to us. "She will accompany Takumi's soul through processing so he will not have to go alone. I will go tend to the humans' souls."

"It should have been me," I sobbed.

Death knelt by me, placing his bony hand on my head. "Your time is not yet here, Daughter. He sacrificed himself for you. It was as fate predicted."

"Fate is a bitch!" Frances shouted and then dropped her head against my arm.

"She can be," Death agreed with a nod. "Do you wish to see your parents?"

"Her grandfather is on his way," one of the chupacabras said.

"I shall leave you then. I am sorry, my daughters," Death whispered and then he disappeared, too.

Grandfather ran to us, Father and Mother right behind him.

"Tsukiko!" Father yelled.

Mother ran to Frances, gathered her up in her arms and hugged her tightly. "I am so sorry."

Grandfather knelt beside me and bowed his head. "What happened?"

"Humans with strange suits and helmets," I whispered. "I came across them fighting Takumi. One of them tried to shoot me, and Takumi jumped between us. He died because of me." Tears blinded me again and sobs wracked my body so hard that I clutched at my stomach and bent over.

"Scour the area!" Grandfather yelled. "See if there are more!"

"Why?" I asked. "It should have been me."

"He died protecting you because he cared for you," Father whispered.

"Because I'm supposed to be special?" I snarled. "Because I'm an elite?"

"Because you were his friend," Mother said, still holding Frances like a child despite her being larger than my mother.

"Come, let's take you home," Father said.

"What about—"

"His body will be dealt with appropriately," Grandfather said.

"Go rest at home and return to school tomorrow with tear-free eyes," Father whispered.

How could I just continue on like nothing had happened?

Takumi had sacrificed himself for me. How could I repay that?

"Takumi would want you to live your life to the fullest," Mother whispered. "So, grieve for your friend and then live your life as you want."

I nodded, giving in and letting them carry me home.

Thanatos, my older brother, processed souls by entering their names into the Book of Death. He wasn't normally the one doing it, but he'd had a fight with Dad who had decided one hundred years of this was an appropriate punishment. I had no idea what their fight had been about, but it had upset my mom enough that she'd isolated herself for a full week.

Thanatos had a dark goatee, black feathered wings, and despite this being his punishment, he smiled as he greeted the souls coming in. He was kind and tried to help everyone die peacefully, if possible.

Normally, a soul would have to wait in line to be entered, but since I was the one bringing in Takumi, he would be processed faster.

"We're almost there," I whispered to the blue light bobbing beside me. I wiped at my face to try to rid the tears that were there, but new ones continued to replace them.

Souls were processed in an adjacent dimension to the realm we lived in. The ground was dirt with the occasional rock, huge mountains surrounded us, their peaks not visible to the normal eye. There were several entrances around the mountains where the souls entered this dimension. The entrances were carved stone arches that said, "Welcome to your afterlife. No pushing or cutting in line. These are entrances only and you may not try to leave through them." From the entrances, the souls bobbed along rock stairways that snaked down the mountainside. Once at the bottom of the mountain, the souls converged into a large area that then funneled them into a single file line. The line started at the base of the mountain and wound all the way along the dirt ground to the gazebo where Thanatos and the Book sat in shade.

We flew up in the air, over the line of souls, and only dropped down once we were right outside the gazebo.

A hell hound stood guard at the entrance, ensuring the souls entered only when it was their turn.

This hell hound was Thanatos's favorite. He'd named it Spot because, "He has a spot of white on the tip of each of his ears."

"Hey, Spot," I whispered and held out my hand.

He licked my hand and then growled at Takumi's soul.

"No, I'm processing this one. Dad's orders," I told Spot.

Spot stopped growling and let out a huff.

"Hey, baby sister. What are..." Thanatos stopped when I turned and he saw my face. He looked at the soul beside me and his mouth opened. "Oh, no. No. Lorie." Thanatos stood. His wings spread behind him a moment before they refolded behind him. Even so, the tips of his wings dragged along the ground due to their enormous size. He wrapped me up in a hug and I wrapped my arms around him, beneath the base of his wings. "Let it out," he whispered.

Thanatos, on top of being kind, had the ability to make you feel safe and unleash emotions you didn't even realize you were feeling.

He rubbed my back and within seconds, the floodgates

opened and I sobbed into his chest. He held me tightly as I broke apart.

"He was my friend. More than a friend. He had pledged his life to me, Than-ny. He loved Kiko and they'll never know if they were a good couple or not. She'll never know what could have been. We spent so much time with him this summer and then he was assigned to us at the school. Now, we'll never hear him laugh, or practice fighting with him, or do any of the fun things he did with us when we were forced to isolate and he guarded us. I just want to hear his voice. One more time. To tell him how much he meant to me. I never told him. I never told him because I know everyone dies and expressing my feelings means opening up to them and accepting them. Dammit, stop using your powers." I pulled back and Thanatos wiped my cheeks with his thumbs. "I hate when you use your powers to make me psychoanalyze myself."

He smiled and stared down at me. "Father is busy. So, I am going to break one of his rules. This one time, okay?"

"What rule?" I asked, sniffling and wiping my nose with the bottom of my shirt.

"One last chance," he whispered.

Beside me, Takumi's soul flashed bright green. Green smoke seeped down from the orb and formed into Takumi's humanoid shape. He took a breath and became fully physical and just as he had looked this morning.

There was no telling how long Thanatos would allow him to be in this form. If Dad or Grandpa showed up, he would have to turn him back into just a soul.

Not wasting the opportunity, I threw my arms around his waist and hugged him. "I'm so sorry. You meant so much to me and I never told you. I'm going to miss you so much."

Takumi hugged me tightly and lightly kissed the top of my head. "I've always known, my little raven. I spent my time with you preparing you to be strong. You three will go far. Never take each other for granted and always watch each other's back. And, always call each other out when your actions aren't in line with your morals."

I pulled back and smiled up at him. "Lecturing me even with your last words. I'd expect nothing less. I love you."

He smiled. "I love you, too."

With a poof of green smoke, he turned back into a bobbing blue soul.

"Come, you can write his name in the Book," Thanatos said.

I hugged him tightly. "Thank you. And never, ever, tell anyone I have emotions."

He patted my back. "Your secret is safe with me."

I stepped up to the desk, grabbed the feather quill, dipped it in the black ink, and with even strokes, wrote Takumi's name in the Book of Death. "Enjoy your afterlife," I whispered. Takumi's soul spun around me once before flying out the exit and towards the entrance to the afterlife. I hadn't seen it yet, so I wasn't sure what it looked like. I hoped it was nice for Takumi.

"Good job, Loralie," Dad said from behind me.

"Dad!" Thanatos and I yelled at the same time.

He looked down at me and said, "Having emotions isn't a bad thing, Loralie. Takumi deserves to be mourned."

I nodded, unsure what to say in response.

"I'll take you back to school. I know you can't shadow travel that far and exiting here is still hard for you," Dad said.

I winced. He'd made me try to exit over one hundred times in one day. I'd ended up sleeping for a week afterwards and Mom had yelled at him. "Thanks."

Thanatos hugged me one more time and I patted Spot on the head before Dad rested his hand on my shoulder. "It gets easier. I am here if you need me."

I hugged him and sighed. "Thanks, Dad."

We returned to school after a funeral for Takumi was held at the Wolf mansion. Loralie didn't cry during the funeral, but that was normal for her. Plus, it allowed her to console Tsukiko and I as we balled and drenched Loralie's shirt in tears. All of the elites had attended, having used Takumi for guard detail for all of us at some point. The hardest part had been seeing Takumi's mother kneeling at his grave silently screaming. I couldn't imagine how much it hurt her to lose her only son. I hoped I never had to find out.

Three weeks later, Baba Yaga was called for an emergency on the other side of the world. Since there were no recent human attacks, she felt it was safe enough and left in her house, the massive chicken legs carrying her far away.

Things started to return to normal.

"Pop quiz!" Mr. Sampson called out from the front of the classroom. He handed a stack of papers to the student at the front of each row and smiled at us. "Hopefully, you kept up on you're assigned reading and paid attention in class. If you did, this will be a piece of stardust cake for you. If you didn't, well, we will discuss that when I hand back your tests tomorrow."

I gulped as the stack made it to me.

"Why do you look nervous?" Loralie asked with a scowl. "You'll ace this no problem."

"We, on the other hand, will likely face whatever punishment Sampson deems necessary," Tsukiko said with a soft whine. Her ears lowered as she looked at the paper. "So doomed."

The quiz was a single page with a very faint outline of a chimera on it. At the top it said, "Label each part of the depicted monster, both internal and external."

"So, doomed," Tsukiko said and dropped her head until her forehead lightly thumped against her desk.

"You have five minutes. Begin!" Mr. Sampson yelled.

Five minutes! That wasn't enough time.

I had done all of the reading and paid attention most of the time in class, but chimeras were one of the monsters I had the most trouble with.

With a deep breath, I focused and started by labeling all of the parts I knew for certain. Labeling those ensured that I, at the very least, got points for those ones. Next, I would turn to the ones I wasn't certain of, but I would label them softly with my pencil so I could easily erase if I was wrong and remembered.

There was no clock or timer and yet it felt like I could hear the seconds as they ticked by.

I should have accepted that watch Dad had offered me. It had been an ugly orange color, but I would have known what time it was and how much time I had left.

Staring at the paper before me, I chewed on my bottom lip. I was missing something, something important. It was on the tip of my brain, but...

"Time!" Mr. Sampson yelled. "Pencils down. Pass the papers up."

Several kids groaned, including Tsukiko. Her ears were drooped super low and she pouted.

Across the room from me, I caught Larson glaring at me. He was a dhampir, but that was all I really knew about him. Loralie knew more about him than I did, but the way he was glaring bothered me. I averted my eyes so he wouldn't catch me staring.

We were used to being glared at simply for being elites. The other monsters thought we had everything handed to us. They didn't understand how much pressure the elites were constantly under or the jobs that the families provided. Tsukiko's family as well. Loralie's family ferried and watched over the souls of the dead. Tsukiko's family kept control of the shapeshifters and also had a huge company that provided protection to monsters who couldn't protect themselves.

His glare was something else. It almost looked...pained.

"Franny," Tsukiko whispered next to my ear.

I leapt to the side, falling out of my seat into the aisle between the desk beside me.

Tsukiko's ears perked, her eyes widened, and her tail raised. "Are you okay? I didn't mean to scare you." She bent down and held out her hand.

I took the offered hand and let her pull me up. "Sorry, was spacing off for a moment."

"What were you thinking about?" Tsukiko asked.

Loralie smirked. "Or, who?" She wiggled her eyebrows and smirked.

I sighed, gathered my notes and book, and shoved everything into my bag. "I'll tell you later."

Tsukiko growled. "Who do I need to bite?"

I rolled my eyes and scoffed. "Down, girl."

We walked towards our next class and I felt eyes on me, glancing behind me, I caught Larson behind us. Still glaring.

I jerked my head back around and swallowed hard.

"You okay?" Loralie asked. "You seem nervous."

"It's nothing," I whispered. "So, what do you think the upperclassmen are going to do for the school festival?"

The week before Samhain, the school held a festival with food booths and crafts you could buy. Only the third and fourth years were allowed to participate in the booths because the school wanted the lowerclassmen to enjoy their time and get ideas for the future when we did it. It was something students raved about even years later. Tsukiko's mom talked about it every year, and apparently came to the school to buy things.

"I hope they have stardust cookies and muffins," Tsukiko said.

Stardust was the most deliciously sweet ingredient ever. Adding it to cakes made them ten times better and muffins at least a hundred times better.

I added stardust to everything I baked. Thankfully, my parents indulged my baking habit and bought lots of stardust. It was getting harder to find, but they still kept it stocked for me.

"I heard there was a class that was going to bring some human foods for us to try," Loralie said.

"Hopefully ones that involve meat. Humans have really yummy meat recipes," Tsukiko said and licked her lips while her tail wagged behind her.

I chuckled. Meat was definitely Tsukiko's vice. She ate anything meat related, no matter what type of meat was involved.

"I'm sure there will be meat dishes," I said, smirking.

CHAPTER 25

The sun set and the wolves howled as the night of the school festival began.

"Come on!" Tsukiko growled, her tail twitching behind her as she paced in front of my door.

I smiled, brushed my hair once more to ensure the tangles were all gone, and then stood. "Okay, I'm ready."

"Finally!" Tsukiko wailed.

"We better head to the food booths first," Frances said, trying and failing to hide her smile. "Everyone have their money?"

I patted my back pocket. "Yep."

"Yes," Tsukiko said and held up a small coin purse with a strap around her wrist.

"Let's go," Frances said cheerily, pulled open the door, and took the lead.

She hadn't told us what had scared her yesterday, but it had to do with our Monsterology class, so I would pay more attention the next class to find out.

"Did you know that humans eat squid?" Tsukiko asked us.

"It's called calamari, right?" I asked. I usually knew more

about humans than my friends due to my family dealing with their deaths.

She nodded. "I really want to try some."

"I heard it can be rubbery if not prepared right," I said.

Frances's nose scrunched up. "Yuck. Who would want to eat rubbery food?"

"Humans are weird," I said and shrugged.

The festival was one of the few things held completely outside since the faculty ensured it was held only once the sunlight was completely gone.

I never understood how vampires could survive at night, since the moonlight was a reflection of the sunlight, but there were many things about monsterkind that made little sense.

It took us several minutes to make it out of the dorm areas and to the field where the food booths were set up.

Immediately, we spotted Sakura, surrounded by male students as she whisked along the food booths and made purchases.

Tsukiko growled and her tail twitched behind her. "Stupid boys."

"At least we won't have to help her carry anything," I said with a smile, trying to ease her irritation.

"True," she grumbled. Instead of going to see her mother, she stopped at the very first booth and ordered one of their featured items.

Frances and I ordered different items so we could all share and try everything.

We stopped at two more booths before our arms were too full and we had to find an empty table to sit and eat at.

"There you three are," Sakura said as she sat beside me, across from Tsukiko.

Four boys carrying a ton of food set the items down on the table in front of us.

"Thank you for your help," Sakura said with a smile.

"How are you, Mother?" I asked, grabbed a round breaded piece of food smothered in sauce, and popped it in my mouth. It was a bit fishy, but was delicious.

"I'm doing well. Make sure you try a bit of everything," she instructed as she grabbed an onion ring out of one of the baskets.

To our left, huge lights turned on, revealing a stage with a band set up. The band was made up of older students I didn't know, and they played rock music with lyrics about hunting under the full moon with a girl they liked. They were really good and I bobbed my head along to the beat while I ate.

"I'll be leaving shortly after going through the shops," Sakura said, looking at Tsukiko. "I won't stay long or bother you."

"Mom, you're not a bother," Tsukiko said. "I do appreciate you being considerate, though. And I'm glad you didn't bring Dad."

She laughed. "Your father hates these events. Mainly because when we were young, I forced him to participate on every event planning committee that existed."

I cringed. "Poor Dad."

Sakura shrugged. "It allowed him to spend time with me and that was what was most important to him."

"Mrs. Okami," Headmistress Gonzalez greeted as she walked to our table. "I'm so glad you could once again join us."

Sakura stood and shook hands with her. "The students always put on the best events and I love supporting them."

"Let's sneak away while she's distracted," Tsukiko whispered before shoving another piece of food I didn't recognize into her mouth.

Most of the food was gone, and we still had a lot to see.

Frances and I nodded our agreement, stood, quickly kissed Sakura on the cheek, and then jogged across the field. We jogged past the stage where a huge crowd had gathered, waved to Ainsley who was talking to a small group of harpies, and finally made it to the shopping booths.

There was a lot more magical items than I expected, including a potion booth.

"Don't get any ideas," Frances said with a scowl as she caught me reading the description on a sleeping potion.

"I was just looking," I lied.

She grabbed my hand and pulled me away from the booth.

I bought some trinkets to give to Frances and Tsukiko, as well as some for my parents and siblings. I would send my families' items by delivery service.

Hours later, exhausted from eating, buying, and partying, we stumbled to our rooms and crashed.

I had always thought I would hate events like this, but I was beginning to learn that some school events weren't so bad. As long as I had my friends with me, anyway.

"Love you," I called through the wall.

"Love you, too," they called back from either side of me.

CHAPTER 26

FRANCES

The festival was even more fun than I had imagined.

Before I knew it, Samhain was upon us.

Normally, Samhain was a time of celebration and joy. We would exchange gifts with the creature we had a crush on and have parties three nights in a row. It was similar to the human's Valentine's Day.

For Tsukiko, Loralie, and I, it was a time of sadness and irritation.

We had no one to give gifts to.

We had no desire to party.

We just wanted to finish our school year and go about our lives.

The pain of Takumi's loss hadn't dulled, even for me.

It felt too soon.

Too recent.

As classes ended the night before Samhain, students chatted excitedly about tomorrow. They discussed the huge party that was going to happen and the rumors of who was going to give who a gift.

We had decided to give no one a gift, not even each other.

"So, who are you three giving gifts to?" Ainsley asked as she walked beside us towards the dorms.

"No one," I answered.

She chuckled. "Oh, you want to keep it a secret. I get it."

"No, we aren't—" I started to explain, but she flew off.

Loralie sighed. "Whatever. Let them think what they want. Hopefully, it will keep them away from us."

"Let's get some food and take it back to the room," Tsukiko said.

"That sounds like an amazing idea," I said and smiled.

The dining hall was surprisingly packed. I hadn't seen so many students in there at one time aside from dinner before.

"What's going on?" I asked a nearby gorgon.

She turned, her snakes lifting above her head to gaze at me. Strangely, she and her snakes had half-closed eyes and looked about to fall asleep. "Everyone is getting snacks so they can stay up and make their gifts for Samhain," she said. She looked us over. "Isn't that why you're here, too?"

"We're here for snacks," I agreed with a nod. She didn't need to know we weren't participating in Samhain.

She turned back around and her snakes lay back on her shoulders, their eyes closing fully.

Was she sick? Most creatures didn't get sick, but maybe she was one of the few who did.

The line moved extra slow due to students taking longer than usual to choose the items they wanted. The staff was calm and collected as they took our orders and I made a mental note to tell Sakura that they should give them a raise for putting up with us.

Once we had our food, we went to Tsukiko's room, turned on mind-numbing television, and pigged out.

All I needed to get through life was delicious food and these two girls.

"I love you two," I whispered.

They looked at me and said, "Love you, too."

The evening of Samhain, we sat in Tsukiko's room, dreading going to classes. We could hear the squealing and feel the excitement from here.

"We could skip classes," Loralie offered.

"They'd report us missing to our parents right away," I argued. "Our parents won't believe any lie we come up with."

Tsukiko growled. "Hopefully, no males will bother us."

"Hopefully," Loralie whispered.

I had little hope of that. The school was big and there was likely at least a lower classman who would give us a gift.

"Let's just go," I said with a sigh.

We were all wearing black pants, a black shirt, and black shoes. Tsukiko had even put black bands to hold her hair back.

"Deep breaths. We can do this," Loralie whispered.

I wasn't sure if she was trying to encourage Tsukiko and me, or herself.

Probably herself.

I opened the door and, on the ground, sat six gifts.

Loralie groaned, grabbed them, and tossed them in the room without even looking to see who they were for or who had left them.

"Happy Samhain!" Ainsley yelled as she flapped past us, down the hallway.

"Happy Samhain," we grumbled beneath our breaths.

We walked out of the dormitory and into a mass of excited creatures.

"This...was a mistake," I whispered.

It was too late, we'd been spotted and several people came up to us, wishing us well and some giving us gifts.

By the time we reached our first classroom, we were irritated and ready to flee.

"This sucks," Loralie whispered and let her head drop to her desk.

"Yeah, it totally does," I agreed.

"Why do you three look so glum? Not get any presents?" Norma asked as she slid into her seat across the room.

"Don't even acknowledge her," I whispered.

"Doesn't surprise me that no one wanted to give you a gift after the way you treated the Evil Three," she added.

I didn't even need to ask who the Evil Three were. It was obviously the guys. The girls liked to give them ridiculous names as they claimed to be their fan club or something else idiotic.

"I'm glad you showed your true colors. Now someone actually deserving of them can get them. Your spell is gone and we can finally make our move," Norma purred.

"Have fun," I said. "Just leave us alone."

Dante came into the classroom, and I immediately dropped my eyes to look at the desk.

"Hey, Dante," Norma crooned. "You look hot today."

"Norma," he greeted.

"I made you this," she said.

I lifted my eyes, but kept my head still, so I could use my hair as a shield to watch them.

She held out a red wrapped box to Dante.

He glanced at me, our eyes meeting even through my veil of hair, and he took the box from her. "Thanks."

I dropped my eyes again, tears burning them.

No. I would not cry.

I had no reason to cry.

"You sure I can't just tear one of her arms off?" Loralie whispered. "She doesn't need both of them."

I sighed. "It would make me feel better."

"Not today," Tsukiko said. "Maybe some day, but you can't tear an arm off today."

"Spoilsport," Loralie muttered.

I let out a short, soft laugh, but it was cut short when Norma laughed at something Dante said.

"Just a few hours left," Tsukiko whispered.

Hopefully, I could make it that long.

CHAPTER 27

LORALIE

Norma's followers were really making me mad. If they said one more thing, I was going to lose my crap and tear one of their arms off to beat them all with it.

Tsukiko was holding it together well, which honestly surprised me. I'd assumed she would have given up by third period.

Frances was dealing with more than Tsukiko or I, though, since Dante kept showing up near her.

I wanted to tell him to back off, but I wasn't sure if that would upset Frances or not.

"What's got you scowling so much on a day that is supposed to be happy?" Bogden asked from beside me.

Phantom goop!

I hadn't heard him approaching. Plus, I'd sat in a different seat than normal to try to avoid him.

"Nothing," I said and started to stand.

He grabbed my wrist and stopped me. "Hey, what's going on? You haven't talked to me in weeks and won't even look at me. What did I do?"

"You didn't do anything," I whispered. "You're better off without me bothering you anyway."

"Bothering me? What are you talking about?" he asked.

I jerked my arm free. "I've got to go." Grabbing my bag, I headed out of the classroom and down the hallway.

"Loralie," Bogden called after me. "Wait."

I wasn't supposed to use my powers during school hours except for emergencies. Well, this was an emergency. An emotional emergency.

I leapt into the nearest shadow and used it to travel to my room.

My two hell hound pups rushed over and licked my hands.

Collapsing to the floor, I let them lick the salty tears from my face.

Maybe I should have let Dad homeschool me after all.

"I don't know why you keep running away from me," Bogden said from outside my door. "I don't know what I did to upset you. I wish you would tell me so I could make it better. I don't want to keep chasing you and risk upsetting you more. So, I'll just leave your gift here. Happy Samhain, Loralie."

Waiting several minutes to be sure he was gone, I opened my door a crack, grabbed the black-wrapped box, and then closed and locked my door.

I sat on the bed and stared at the box.

Bogden had gotten me a Samhain gift.

I hadn't expected that.

I was dying to know what was inside, but at the same time, I didn't want to open it.

With a groan, I flopped back onto my bed and closed my eyes. Maybe a nap would help.

My nap was immediately interrupted by Tsukiko and Frances barging into my room.

My ferocious hell hounds yipped excitedly and rolled onto their backs for belly rubs.

"We've got a problem," Frances said.

I looked at them both and saw that each held a package.

"Rathik and Dante?" I guessed.

They nodded.

I pointed at the one Bogden had left me. "Bogden."

We carried our packages to the table and set them in the center, then backed up and glared at them.

"We're not opening them, right?" Tsukiko asked.

"We are not opening them," I said with a definitive nod.

"Well, I'm fine not opening them, but we cannot give them back. That'd be incredibly rude," Frances whispered.

I agreed with a nod. "So, we put them in a box and hide them in the closet?" I suggested.

Tsukiko agreed with a nod, went to her room, and then returned with a box large enough to fit the three inside. We carefully put them in the box, then taped it up like we were trying to keep a creature from escaping.

Then, Frances carefully put the box into the closet and closed the door.

"There," I said with an exhale.

"Out of sight, out of mind," Tsukiko said and flopped down onto my bed.

"Well, mostly," Frances murmured.

"We're taking the rest of the night off," Tsukiko said. "I can't deal with them anymore."

"She almost tore off some guy's arm when he tried to give her some chocolates," Frances chuckled.

"Time for naps?" I suggested. They had interrupted my attempt, and I was tired.

"Naps," they agreed.

We climbed onto the bed, snuggled down together beneath the blankets, and fell into a deep sleep.

"What are you three doing?" Ainsley gasped.

I groaned and pulled the covers up tighter. "Go away."

"It's Samhain! Why are you guys hiding? It's time to celebrate!" she chirped.

I could hear her prancing around the room. Her talons clicked on the tile in the bathroom before she returned near us, her feathers brushed my nose and almost made me sneeze.

"You had ten packages at your doors. I brought them in so no one could steal them," she continued.

"We aren't going out," Tsukiko said. "Just let us sleep."

"It's almost midnight. Everyone is heading to the party. You guys can't skip it," she said with a guffaw.

"We can and we are," I said. "Seriously, Ainsley, we aren't coming. Just tell everyone we're sick or something."

She chirped so softly and sadly that it almost broke my heart. "Okay," she whispered. "I'm sorry."

The door closed with a whisper soft click and the room grew silent once again.

"We hurt her feelings, didn't we?" I guessed.

"Yeah, but she'll get over it," Tsukiko said. "Let's eat and then we can watch something."

We sat together on the bed, watching the television, and eating food.

I didn't like that I had hurt Ainsley's feelings, but this was for the best.

Staying away from everyone was definitely for the best.

CHAPTER 28

FRANCES

Having a blindfold, gag, and handcuffs put on you first thing when you wake up was not something I ever thought I would have to experience.

As I was carried out of the room, I struggled, kicking and flailing while also screaming around the gag.

I could hear lots of commotion, but no one was talking. There were a lot of grunts and distressed muffled sounds, though.

"To the room with this one," someone said.

I kicked out towards the voice, my legs the only thing I could move at the moment.

A cold piece of metal pressed against my neck. "Unless you want to try to find a new head, monster, shut up and stay still."

I drew in a breath and fear caused me to freeze.

Humans.

Oh, gods. Oh, gods.

Where were Loralie and Tsukiko?

Were they alright?

What were we going to do?

How had they gotten onto campus?

How had they managed to get us like this?

A door opened and hot sunlight covered my body.

Of course. They waited until the morning after Samhain to attack us, when we would be exhausted from staying up late and our guard would be down.

But how were they subduing the creatures with powers? Creatures like Dante and Rathik?

Why had Baba Yaga left?

The scent of blood and death filled my nostrils as we continued to walk and I tried not to gag.

What had happened?

I both wanted to see and didn't at the same time.

The human carrying me tossed me on the ground, my butt hitting the hard floor, but thankfully missed my tailbone.

I grunted in pain and sat up, backing away from where the human had been.

I scooted until I touched a warm body, and then tried to move away, but heat from above my head made me stop.

Was that Dante?

"Frances," Dante whispered. "It's okay. I'm right here." His fingers brushed mine, and I gripped his as much as I could with my bound hands. With the gag in, I couldn't respond to him, but there wasn't really anything I could say anyways.

"Keep an eye on that one," an unfamiliar voice said. "He shouldn't be able to use his fire, but I still wouldn't trust him."

"What about the girl beside him? That's Frankenstein's kid, right?" Another unfamiliar voice asked.

"She's harmless. She's supposedly smart, but how smart can a monster be? If she starts acting up, just burn her a bit. I've heard she's scared of fire."

"You keep your filthy human hands off her," Dante snapped.

"Oh, ho? Tough guy, huh? Got a thing for the zombie chick? That's useful information," one of the voices said.

A door shut and Dante sighed behind me. "I don't know how they got in or got to us all so quickly, but it looks like most of the school is split up into smaller groups and they're guarding us pretty well. They used some potion that made it difficult to use our powers."

He'd said difficult, not impossible.

I tried to ask about my friends, but the stupid gag wasn't helping me talk at all.

"I haven't seen Tsukiko or Loralie," he whispered. "They're still bringing people in, though. So, maybe they'll be brought in soon."

Tears burned the corners of my eyes and I sniffled, trying to stop them.

Dante rested his chin atop my head and said, "It's okay. I won't let them hurt you. We'll figure a way out of this. Or, the elites will come and save us."

I hoped so.

I really really hoped so.

"Hey, move back from her," one of the humans snapped.

Dante growled, but scooted back. He kept our fingers touching, though behind my back, which the human probably couldn't see.

I hoped this wouldn't be the last time we touched.

I hoped my friends were okay.

Lucifer, below, save us, please.

CHAPTER 29

LORALIE

Before I could process what had happened, my two hell hounds yelped in pain, a burning liquid was poured down my mouth, and I was bound in strong restraints.

"That was easier than I thought," an unfamiliar voice said.

I inhaled and immediately snarled.

Humans.

I tried to shadow travel, but my powers weren't working.

What was going on?

One of the humans picked me up and tossed me over their shoulder.

I kicked and flailed, trying to get them to drop me so I could run, but someone punched me in the face, knocking me unconscious.

When I awoke, I sat in the middle of a bright field, trees far away, so no shadows were near me.

There were ten other students, most those who could use shadows to fight. They were all bound by the hands and feet, and then hogtied together to prevent us from escaping.

They must have bound me the same way while I was knocked out.

I looked around, fear clawing at my chest, but I didn't see Tsukiko or Frances.

That was both reassuring and not at the same time.

Were they safe? Had they managed to escape? Or were they being held somewhere else.

Two warm fingertips pressed into my back. I turned and met Bogden's eyes. He was also bound and here.

He scooted closer, his eyes burning bright, and rested his forehead against mine. "Are you okay?" He asked telepathically.

"I'm unhurt," I responded the same way.

"Don't worry, I won't let them hurt you."

"What is going on?" I asked.

"Humans attacked, using a potion that prevents us from using our powers. That's all I know at this point. It seems like they're moving us to places where our powers are even less useful."

"Can you communicate with your mom?" I asked hopefully.

"No."

Crap. There went that idea.

"We'll figure something out. Let's just rest and save up our energy. Hopefully, this potion will wear off soon and we can attack them."

I liked that plan.

I pulled back from him, realizing we must have looked like we were consoling each other as a couple or something. Scooting a bit back from him, I lay on my side and closed my eyes. If I was lucky, Dad would try to dream walk with me and I could warn him of what was happening. He didn't do it often, but I could hope.

Bogden scooted closer, rolled onto his back, and wiggled his bound fingertips towards me.

Indecisiveness filled me, but I ultimately gave in, reaching forward to touch our fingertips together.

"I know you're upset with me or something, but this is beyond us. We need to work together to save everyone. Okay?" His voice filled my head and made my heart beat faster. This was the first time he had communicated telepathically with me.

"Okay," I agreed because he was right. This went way beyond my feelings for him or our inability to date. This was about saving my friends. This was about saving everyone at the school.

And killing the humans.

The sun pressed down onto me, making me sweat, and making me more uncomfortable than I already was bound up and lying on the ground.

Sleep evaded me for a bit, but Bogden moved closer, our fingers entwined, and I drifted off to sleep.

Unfortunately, Dad didn't show up in any of my dreams. That made me worry because that likely meant he didn't even know about the attack yet.

How long would it be before an outsider found out? If the humans had killed all of the chupacabras and wolfmen, then no one would be able to report to an outsider that we were under attack.

How had these stupid humans gotten us all under control so quickly?

The only answer was one that made my skin crawl and fury fill me.

Someone on the inside was working with them.

But why? What would a creature gain by working with humans?

They had to know that they couldn't trust these vile creatures, right? Humans would make promises and then turn right around and stab you in the back. Or, they'd make you a promise that would backfire.

It just didn't make sense.

Was it the werewolves? Were they really so tired of being under the Okami's control that they would stoop to something so low as this?

If it was them, they would be in for a rude awakening when Sakura and Tanjiro tore out their throats for putting us in danger.

Where were Tsukiko and Frances? Were they okay?

I couldn't stop thinking about my best friends and hoping they were fine.

I prayed to Satan and any other dark god who might be listening to protect them.

I couldn't take another friend's soul to the Underworld.

Not yet.

The memory of taking Takumi's soul was still too fresh and too painful.

I didn't want to ferry anymore souls this decade.

CHAPTER 30

TSUKIKO

The stench of humans filled my nostrils, but worse than that was the stench of death and blood from creatures.

I'd awoken, bound, blindfolded, and in a dark and damp area on a cold rock floor.

There were others around me, some nagas, gorgons, and harpies, to name a few.

Specifically, I smelled Rathik, Ainsley, and Antoine.

I managed to get the blindfold off by rubbing my face on the ground, but there wasn't enough light to see very far.

"Ainsley," I whispered.

"Tsukiko?" she whispered back.

"Are you alright?" I asked.

She sobbed and then I heard scratching sounds right before she pressed her dirty face to my shoulder. "I'm so scared."

Her right eye was swollen shut and blood dripped from a cut on her forehead.

"What happened?" I gaped.

"I woke up before they could get the potion in my mouth and fought back. They overpowered me, though, and forced me to drink it." She sniffled and inched closer. "I can't shift and I think my right wing is broken."

I would tear apart every single human here.

"It's okay. We're together now. I'll protect you," I promised her.

"Tsukiko?" Rathik whispered.

"Here," I whispered back.

He scooted to my other side and rested his chin atop my head. "Oh, thank the dark gods. You're alive."

The relief I heard in his voice was surprising considering our recent interactions.

"Are you injured?" I asked.

"No, but I can't shift into my snake form," he hissed. "I'm stuck with human legs."

I tried to access my wolf, but it was like a cage surrounded her and kept her at bay.

"I can't shift either," I admitted with a whine.

"I'm here," Rathik whispered. "Don't worry."

I wasn't worried about myself.

"Frances? Loralie?" I asked.

"I haven't seen them," Ainsley whispered.

"Me neither. I heard one of the humans whispering about other rooms. They might have separated you guys," Rathik whispered.

"Was this an inside job then?" I asked. Very few people knew to keep us separated. I hadn't thought any of the students here knew that either.

"I think so," Rathik said, his chin moving in a nod atop my head.

"Antoine?" I called softly.

"Tsukiko?" he asked from somewhere behind me.

"Over here," I called.

"Hey! No talking!" a human yelled.

We all silenced and stilled.

After several minutes, I heard soft, slow movement as Antoine inched closer to us.

"Is this the werewolves?" I asked him, point blank.

"I don't know," he admitted. "I'm not part of that circle. I'm devoted to your family, so they won't discuss their business around me."

Made sense. They wouldn't want someone who still supported us to find out about their coup plans and risk them being thwarted.

"I hope it isn't them," I whispered.

"Me too," Antoine muttered. "Are you hurt?" he asked and scooted closer, pressing his nose to my cheek.

"Back off," Rathik hissed and pulled me back away from Antoine with his knees.

"What the—" Antoine asked, but went silent. "I'm not after her, dude. She's my friend. That's it."

I pushed away from Rathik. "Knock it off. This is not the time for stupid male games. We need to figure out a plan and—"

Something hit me in the jaw, stunning me into silence and knocking me on my back.

"I said shut up!" the human from earlier yelled.

Rathik and Antoine tried to move, but I barked, "No," and they settled back down.

"No more talking or I'll separate you into individual cells. Do you understand?" the human asked.

"Yes," I said, suppressing a growl.

"Good."

On the cold floor, I thought over my options.

If Loralie couldn't access the shadows, then we had no way to communicate. With Frances away, she couldn't formulate a plan for us.

I didn't even know if they were alive.

No! No, I refused to believe they were dead.

I would have felt it if they were killed.

No one knew our secret, but the three of us would know if one of us was killed.

They were alive. I just had no idea where.

"We need to get out of here," I whispered. "Regroup. Let's each think of a plan and in a few minutes, we'll see if we've come up with anything that might work."

Something had to work.

There had to be some way to get out of here.

I wouldn't give up. Not when my friends needed me. Not when my family was out there.

I would escape and find my sisters.

One way or another.

There were so many smells down here that I couldn't say for certain how many humans there were guarding us.

We knew there was at least two, but there could be more outside of the room, just waiting to attack.

I didn't want to endanger Ainsley or any of the other students by recklessly attacking the humans.

With no knowledge of the outside situation, no weapons, not even my own claws to use, we were pretty much stuck here.

None of us could guess the humans' motives either, since they had captured us, but they weren't killing us or even torturing us.

"What if they're going to use us to prove to the humans that we do exist?" Rathik whispered.

"We just won't change if that's the case," Antoine said.

I shook my head. "There are some, like the gorgons, who don't shift and won't be able to hide their serpent bodies. Not to mention the trolls and ogres."

"Oh, right," Antoine mumbled.

"What about the teachers?" Ainsley asked. "They can't have taken out the teachers and the guards all so quickly, right?"

"Their armor is incredibly strong," I whispered and then swallowed hard as the memories of Takumi surfaced. "My claws can't tear through it. And they have some strange ability to suppress their scents."

"That part has to be magic," Rathik said. "I can't see any scientific way for them to accomplish that."

I shrugged. "I'm not much of a scientist. Frances might know, but that's not my strong suit."

"The door to this dungeon is solid metal, infused with iron, silver, and sea prism stones," Ainsley whispered.

The door was basically impenetrable for a creature. The silver would burn Antoine and me, the sea prism stones would weaken Ainsley and Rathik, and the iron would burn any fae creatures.

This must have been where they kept students or teachers who got out of control.

"So, we just wait?" Ainsley asked.

The human guarding us approached. He had been making a slow circuit around the room and we rushed to speak while he was on the opposite side.

As he grew closer, we grew silent and still.

I tracked him with my eyes as well as I could in the dark.

He carried a weapon of some kind.

Was it a normal gun? Or did they have special bullets? How much did they know about us and our weaknesses?

There were too many unknowns!

Once he was on the other side of the room, Rathik moved closer to me, resting his chin on my shoulder to whisper in my ear. "We can't attack them without knowing what type of weapons they have. The only way to find out is to get attacked, but how can we do that without dying?"

"That is a stupid plan," I growled at him. "No one is getting attacked just so we can figure out what type of gun they have.

We just need to bide our time and see what happens. If they try to take one of us, then we attack as one."

"Fine," Antoine said.

"Yeah," Ainsley said. "I don't want to get shot, but I won't let anyone die because I was too cowardly to fight back."

"Spread the word," I whispered. "Let's get all of the other students on the same page."

"On it," Ainsley and Antoine said at the same time.

I started to move, too, but Rathik stopped me. "Tsukiko, I don't know what I did to upset you, but I'm sorry. I don't want you to be mad at me. I know you've had a lot going on and your life isn't easy in general."

"I'm not mad at you," I whispered immediately. "You didn't do anything wrong. It's just...we aren't meant to be together. My fear of you won't decrease, no matter what we try. We tried for weeks and nothing helped. I wish there was another way, but there isn't. You and I just have to accept that we—"

Rathik interrupted me with a kiss that had my blood boiling with energy. He pulled back and whispered, "We will figure something out. I'm not giving up on us."

"There is no us," I said and sighed. "Why are you so stubborn? We've never even been on a date or anything. There are lots of other females out there who would love to date you. Give them a chance. You shouldn't need to change for someone to be happy. Even if I did like you that much, which I have never said, there's nothing for us to pursue."

Before he could respond, I scurried away from him and towards the nearby other students to fill them in on the plan.

I liked Rathik a lot, more than I should, but I wasn't going to let him know that. He deserved to be happy and trying to date me would not make him happy. It would just end with us both being miserable.

I would do whatever I could to keep him from being miserable.

Including making myself miserable.

From what we could tell based on our group, they had split the students up by power type. Or something along those lines.

We still had no idea what their motive was or what they were doing to any of the other students.

I just knew that Loralie and Tsukiko were alive and that was really all that mattered at the moment.

Dante moved closer and closer to me as time passed and he held my hand fully now.

I wanted the stupid gag out of my mouth or the blindfold off, but I didn't dare try to do either of those things. I couldn't risk Dante getting injured protecting me for doing something so simple and stupid to piss off the humans.

The humans weren't talking, which bothered me immensely.

What were they planning to do with us?

They were keeping us in small groups, which meant there were likely many humans here. That thought alone was incredibly unreassuring.

I wanted to speak to Dante, to say something, but the damn gag wouldn't loosen.

"The next time the human moves across the room, I'll take out your gag, okay?" Dante whispered in my ear. The heat from his hair grew stronger and I swallowed my fear down.

He wouldn't hurt me.

I gave him a brief nod.

After a few minutes, he pulled the gag out of my mouth.

I rolled my jaw around and licked my dry lips. "Thank you," I whispered.

He pressed his forehead to mine and I instinctively jerked away. He whispered, "I promise, my flames will not hurt you. Ever."

"How do you know?" I asked.

"Because I control who it burns," he whispered. "It is the very first thing that Phoenix children are taught."

"I'm sorry I can't be less scared. I try to be fearless, but I'm not like Loralie or Tsukiko. Fire is instinctively terrifying for me. No matter how much I try to get over it, I just can't. When I feel the heat from the flames I want to run away as far as I can. I try so hard to be close to you, but—"

He rested his head atop mine and said, "It's okay. The fact that you try at all is enough for me. I swear, by every dark god in existence, that my flames will never ever burn you."

"I'll try," I whispered.

His lips pressed to my cheek. "That's enough for me."

Heat bloomed upon my cheeks, and I turned away from him.

What was I doing? I couldn't be with him!

This was hopeless. This was insane.

I was insane.

He removed my blindfold and I smiled up at him.

"What are we going to do?" he asked softly.

"We're going to wait for Loralie to contact us and tell us

what the situation is. Then, we will figure out a plan," I whispered back.

"No whispering!" one of the humans yelled.

Stupid humans. It was definitely time to take this world back. To cull the human race and let monsters take back over. Once and for all.

The trees' shadows moved closer to us, slowly, as the hours passed.

In just another two hours' time, I could roll over and use the shadows to travel.

The potion was slowly wearing off, which made me excited.

Up until they started coming around, making the students drink more of the potion.

"I can't drink it," I whispered to Bogden. "If I do, I won't be able to shadow travel."

His eyes widened. "You're going to leave?"

I shook my head. "I'm just going to scout things out."

"If they realize you're missing, they'll probably start hurting us to find out where you went," he whispered.

"That's why I'm just going to scout," I explained. "I'll scout a bit and come back, so they won't realize I'm gone."

"We'll need to create a distraction," he said, his eyes dropping to the ground as he thought up a plan. "Or, we need to just get our side under control while you find out what we can do."

"What do you mean?" I asked.

"If we can get control of our side here, then if we know

where our enemies are from your scouting, we can formulate a plan of attack," he explained.

The human drew nearer, a silver bottle that looked familiar in his hand.

"I'll create a distraction and you go, okay?" Bogden whispered.

"Don't get hurt," I ordered him.

He smirked. "Don't worry about me, Lor. Just worry about yourself."

Before I could add more, he jumped to his feet and stalked towards the human.

"Sit down," the human warned.

The other human guarding us stood on the outside of the circle, but he drew closer as Bogden continued to advance on the one giving us the potion.

A few of the other students looked from me to Bogden and seemed to understand what was happening, and they stood as well.

Slowly, I backed up, trying not to draw the attention of the humans as they focused on Bogden and the others.

"Sit back down or you'll regret it," the human with the potion ordered Bogden.

Bogden snapped his fingers and a black hole opened up right beside the human with the bottle.

"Now!" Bogden yelled.

I hopped closer to the trees' shadows and leapt in without looking back.

Please stay safe, I silently begged him.

Once in the shadows, I traveled around the school, mentally noting where the humans were, and then returned to Bogden.

I sighed in relief when I saw everyone was untied and had moved to the shade of the trees. The humans were gone, but I didn't care to know what had happened. Likely, someone had eaten them.

He rushed to me and started untying my binds. "What did you find?"

"They have us separated into over a dozen different groups. There are also five sets of three on perimeter patrol. By my count, there are at least forty humans. I wasn't able to find Frances or Tsukiko, which means they must have more groups in odd places, which increases the number of humans, too."

"Anyone hurt?" he asked.

I shook my head. "From what I can tell, they're just keeping us hostage."

"Why?" he whispered and began to pace. "What do they think they'll accomplish?"

"The only thing that I can think of is to expose us to the humans," I whispered. "But wouldn't they have done that by now? What are they waiting for?"

"Could be ransom," a Lamia witch I didn't know said from the trees. "They might want our families to pay them."

That was a definite possibility. Our families were old and had invested heavily in the human world to keep us, well, rich. Not every creature was rich, but most of the ones who went to this academy were.

"We do have several very wealthy families here," Bogden said.

"This definitely feels like an inside job," I whispered.

"Or at least done with insider knowledge," Bogden agreed.

"Who? Who would benefit from this?" I had my suspicions, but I didn't want to voice them.

"I'm not sure, but whoever they are, they are going to pay for this," Bogden promised.

"I should do some more scouting," I said.

"Don't reveal yourself or get caught," he urged. "Just find

out the situation, try to locate all the groups, and come back. We can map out the locations and that will help us make our plan of action."

I nodded. "Understood."

He opened his mouth, but then closed it again without saying anything.

I took a breath and went back into the shadows.

I was beginning to lose hope, to worry that Loralie was in more danger than I was.

Then, her head popped up between Dante and me. "They've separated us into dozens of groups. There are over a hundred humans holding us hostage. We don't know the purpose yet. Stay docile until we find out anything else. Don't try to play the hero."

"Did they not give you the potion?" Dante asked.

"We defeated our humans before they gave us the second dose," she explained. She looked up at me and said, "Frankie, please don't endanger yourself. I'm going to get us free, okay? Just trust me to take care of things."

I nodded. "Okay. I promise."

"Love you," she whispered.

"Love you, too."

She disappeared and I dropped my head forward.

Dante scooted over so my head rested against his shoulder. "See? Things are in motion. We just need to wait for our assignments."

"Dante, the only logical explanation for this is that they are holding us for ransom and that someone on the inside is, or has, helped them. It could be someone in this room. We need to keep quiet about Loralie and our plan, so they don't help them further."

"You really think another creature would help the humans?" He asked.

I nodded.

"Wow, that's awful to think about," he whispered.

Not really. I knew many who defected to the humans. Look at the werewolves for just one example.

For some reason, though, I didn't think this was the werewolves doing. There was nothing that gave heed to that, but that was my gut feeling and I always trusted my gut.

"Did you like your gift?" Dante asked. "You never told me."

I grimaced. "I didn't open it."

He jerked away from me. "Did you throw it away?"

I shook my head vigorously. "No, no, of course not. I just didn't open it."

"Why not?"

How could I explain this without being rude?

"We aren't compatible," I whispered. "You are better off with someone else. Someone who isn't terrified of your fire. I'm fine with being friends with you, but doubt it could ever go beyond that. How could it when I can't stay near you for very long?"

"You're near me now," he whispered.

"Only because you're holding back your flames. You can't do that all the time. You are a phoenix. You are a being of fire. The instant you go all flame bird, I'm going to freak out and run away. That is no way to live. That is not the image I envision when I picture my ideal relationship. Plus, we're so young. I'm sure you'll lose interest in me soon." I said the last sentence in a tiny voice.

"What do you envision as your ideal relationship?" he asked softly.

"Cuddling while watching shows. Walking along the beach together. Attending family events hand in hand," I whispered. Sadly, I could picture all of those things with him, but I could also see myself running in terror, too.

He was not the problem.

I was.

He didn't respond, which I hoped meant he was going to drop it and accept that we didn't have a future together.

I could never be around his family. Plus, I couldn't have kids with him. I would drop the baby the first time it went all flame-bird. That would mortify me for life.

That would destroy me.

After visiting at least eight of the different groups of students, one thing became clear. I had no idea what the humans were planning.

None of the students were being hurt. They weren't taking our DNA. They weren't even taking pictures.

Everyone was split into groups with their hands tied, some were blindfolded, some also gagged, and there were at least two guards with them.

The barrier felt strange and I didn't want to even try passing through it. Dad always told me to trust my instincts and I was going to avoid getting near the barrier as much as possible.

What the heck were they planning?

Their weapons looked like rifles, but I knew very little about weapons, so I wasn't too sure. I really should have paid more attention when Dad was teaching me about weapons.

I hadn't found Tsukiko yet, but she was still alive, so I had to be content with that for the moment. Hopefully, she had some students with her that could provide backup if she needed it.

Dark gods, I hoped she didn't need it. She was rash and

impulsive, but she rarely attacked without a plan. Knowing her, the alpha instinct to protect everyone had kicked in, which meant she wouldn't recklessly attack the humans because she wouldn't want the others to get hurt for something she did.

My biggest question was, where were all of our teachers? That was bothering me most of all. I had seen a few of the guards' bodies around the campus, but none of the teachers.

Hiding in the shadows of a tree at the entrance of the grounds, I looked at the buildings before me.

If I were a bunch of stinky, conniving humans, where would I take the teachers?

They definitely weren't in the first two sub-levels because I had checked those thoroughly. Even the catacombs and graveyard.

Lifting my eyes, I looked at the window of the head-mistress's office. Her office was large enough to fit all of the teachers, plus ten or so humans. That had to be where they were. Or the cafeteria. Or the auditorium.

No, my gut was telling me it was the headmistress's office. Mom always told me to trust my gut, so that was my best bet.

But there was a lot of light in that room. Would there be enough shadow for me to hide in? Or even get up there with? Since the headmistress's office was in the main building, every-thing was above ground and there were lights and windows everywhere. It was the brightest building in the entire school.

With Dad's help, I had been practicing traveling by shadows a lot. I wasn't able to travel too far at once, but I could travel two or three floors at a time along the shadows of mold-ings and drains.

The headmistress's office was on the fourth floor and faced the sunset, so it was full of sun at the moment.

The other side of the building might work, but I'd have to be really careful not to get caught while moving through the rooms and hallways once I got inside the building.

If I had the girls with me, I could do it easily, but I couldn't risk taking them away from their locations and endangering the others.

Bogden had told me to just scout and come back, but I needed to scout this room.

I needed to find the teachers. Our teachers were powerful and if freed, they could be the turning point in our battle.

Chewing on my lip, I weighed my decisions.

The longer I left Tsukiko and Frances where they were, the more they would worry and want to fight their way out.

If I hurried too much, I would get sloppy and get caught.

I could just get caught anyway. I had used a lot of power and I honestly wasn't sure how much more I had.

Maybe I should go back to Bogden and try to bring him with me? No, I didn't have enough power for that. Not until I rested for a bit.

Should I rest first and let my power rejuvenate?

I growled softly at my indecisiveness.

A human guard nearby turned in my direction.

With wide eyes, I jumped from shadow to shadow across the grounds to the back of the building.

There were four guards on the backside of the building, all armed and facing away from the building.

It would have saved me a lot of power if I could have walked up to the building to a shadow, but I had to hurry.

With a deep breath, and a prayer to any of the dark gods who might be listening, I leapt from the shadow I was in at the base of a shrub to the side of the wall beside the drain pipe.

I was going to do this and I wasn't going to get caught.

I could do this.

I was Death's daughter!
Death incarnate.
I could do this!
I hoped…

CHAPTER 36

TSUKIKO

My girls were still alive, but that was all I knew. As the hours continued to pass, my worry grew.

If Loralie did manage to get free and she was shadow traveling around the school looking for us or scouting, which I knew would be her plan, she was going to drain herself quickly.

I knew she had been building up her stamina, but there was no way she could keep traveling all around the school for hours on end.

"What are you growling about?" Rathik asked softly.

Not realizing I was growling, I stopped and felt my cheeks warm. "I'm just worried about Loralie and Frances."

"I'm sure they're okay," he whispered.

"Of course we're okay," Loralie whispered behind me.

I spun around and glared at the dark shape that was her head poking up from the ground behind me. "What took you so long?"

I didn't even need to have light to know she rolled her eyes at me.

"That stupid door made it almost impossible to get in here. I found a crack in the wall that I slipped through, though. Also, I'm fine, thank you for asking."

In the dark, I almost let the few tears of relief in my eyes free, but I didn't want to chance anyone smelling them. "Did you find Frances?"

"She's fine."

"Status?" I asked.

As Loralie updated me on her findings, the hair on my neck stood on end. This was not something I had ever seen humans do before. What were they waiting for?

"The teachers are all in cages in the headmistress's office, but they don't appear to be injured or drugged aside from that potion they keep making everyone drink," Loralie whispered. "I think if I can free them, we could figure out how to defeat the humans."

"Why didn't you travel to your parents?" Rathik asked.

Loralie sighed, brought her entire body up out of the shadow, and pressed her back against mine. "I spent too much of my energy trying to find everyone and scouting the situation out. Plus, there is a weird magical barrier up that made me uneasy when I got near it. I'm not sure I want to try to pass through it."

She leaned against me heavily, giving away just how spent she was. "Take a nap," I ordered her. "It's too dark for the humans to see you."

Her soft snores were the only response.

Relief surged through me at knowing my friends were safe. Well, as safe as they could be.

Fear also flowed within me as I thought about the humans and tried to figure out who might be helping them.

It was someone who could erect a magical barrier. That got rid of the werewolves and a lot of the other races.

Was it a student? Or was it one of their parents?

It had to be a student. They had to have gotten the intelligence that they needed to split the three of us up from another student.

I wanted to find them and introduce them to my claws.

"Kiko," Loralie whispered.

"Hm?"

"Don't do anything stupid."

I chuckled. "Go back to sleep. I'm not moving until you wake up."

There hadn't been any noise that suggested the humans had radios on them. And with my hearing, I would have been able to hear even an earpiece.

If we took out the humans guarding us, would they be able to alert the others somehow? Even if we took them out, how were we supposed to get past that damn door?

"Potion time," one of the humans, the one who had hit me, said.

Loralie jerked awake. "I need to get you out of here."

"They do a head count when they give us the potion," I whispered.

Loralie bounced her leg as she thought.

"Did your guards have radios?" I asked.

"Not that I've seen. Plus, I doubt they could use them with how deep we are underground," she whispered. "Time to fight?"

With a deep breath, I calmed myself, focused on my inner animal, and pulled. It was sluggish, but I was able to lengthen and thicken my nails into claws and my teeth into fangs.

"Fight," I growled.

"What are you planning?" Rathik hissed. "You agreed that we couldn't—"

"Drink up, snakeboy," the human ordered.

"Mist and slash," I growled at Loralie.

She snapped her fingers, giving me the sign, and as she

covered the human's head in a cloud of black shadows, I used my claws to cut his throat. Unable to cry out and alert the other guard, he fell silently.

"Round two," Loralie said and began crawling through the other students towards the second human guard.

He didn't know what hit him.

"That all of them?" Loralie asked.

"Yes," Rathik said. "There aren't any more in this room."

"Let me scout on the other side of the door and then if it is safe, I will open it," Loralie said and disappeared before I could object.

I growled my frustration.

"Do you guys practice combined fighting attacks like that often?" Antoine asked.

"That was the coolest thing ever. I wish I had been able to see it better, though. Stupid darkness," Ainsley muttered.

"Is anyone hurt?" I asked just loud enough for everyone to hear.

"No," most said.

"There are a lot of humans around the campus, so for now, we are just going to move everyone into the cell on the opposite side of the hallway." That one didn't have the same type of door, so they could escape easily if needed.

"Where are you going to go?" Antoine asked.

"Loralie and I are going to try to free the teachers. Once we know it is safe, we will come back for you all," I said.

"You two are not going alone," Rathik hissed. "You can't fight all those humans."

"We aren't going to fight them all," I said and rolled my eyes. "We are going to free the teachers, so they can instruct us what to do."

"Who made you the leader?" Norma snapped.

She was always trying to start trouble. It was time to put a stop to it. Marching right up into her face, I asked, "You want to walk out there, get killed, and risk getting every other student on campus killed? Or do you want to sit down, shut up, and let us handle it?"

The tension built, but after a moment she scoffed and walked away. "I won't be crying when they toss your corpse into a fire."

The door opened and Loralie said, "If they kill us, you have no hope of surviving, trampy vamp."

Norma flipped her hair as she stomped past Loralie, not bothering to respond.

"Ready?" Loralie asked.

"Take me with you," Rathik insisted.

"It will drain me too much to take you, too," Loralie said softly. "I'll keep her safe. Promise."

He hissed and slithered down the hall.

My entire body froze as fear of his form consumed me.

Loralie set her hand on my shoulder and said, "Let's go rescue our favorite patchwork doll."

The joke should have cheered me up, Frances hated when we called her that, but a sense of dread filled me instead.

What if this was the last time I saw Rathik?

And all I could do was stare in fear.

CHAPTER 37

FRANCES

"Psst," Loralie whispered behind me.

I turned my head and stared at her mouth and nose sticking up from the small shadow my body made on the floor. "What are you doing?"

"It's too bright in here. I need a shadow so I can transport Tsukiko and I inside fully," she explained.

"If we sit side by side, will that give you enough shadow?" Dante asked.

Her lips pulled up in a wide smile. "See, I knew he was more than just pretty. We're going to teleport and then take out your guards. 'Kay?"

"Stop talking!" one of the guards yelled.

Slowly, so we didn't draw attention to ourselves, we pivoted until the entire side of our body was pressed together. He was so warm that I almost jerked away, but I held my place.

Tsukiko and Loralie popped up behind us.

"Evening, gents," Loralie greeted and waved at the guards.

They aimed their guns at her and Tsukiko. "Who are you? How'd you get here?"

"Did anyone report losing students?" The other guard asked and reached for his belt where a handheld radio hung.

"Kiko, left. Lor, right," I ordered and charged down the center.

Kiko leapt over the students sitting between us and the guard on the left. Loralie flew around the side of the room and by the time she reached the guard on the right, her scythe had materialized in her hand.

As they cut them down, I snatched the radios from their waists.

"When did you learn to move like that?" Dante asked.

We ignored him. Now was not the time to get into it.

"Everyone stay in the room and don't make much noise. We aren't sure the routes their guards are taking yet and we don't want to alert them that we aren't being watched," Loralie ordered everyone.

"What is going on?" Himari, a tiny female fox with seven tails, asked.

"The humans have taken over the school. They have the teachers locked up, but we're working on a plan to free them. We aren't sure what the humans' plan is since they aren't taking pictures, torturing, or experimenting on anyone. There is a magical barrier around the school and we aren't sure what type of barrier it is, so we are hesitant to try to break through it," Tsukiko answered.

"I could find out," Larissa, a witch, said. "I just need to hover my hand near it."

Loralie looked at me. "Frances?"

"It would be helpful information to have. We are running pretty blind not knowing what their plan for us is," I said. "Can you get her there without being spotted?"

"Yes," Loralie said with a nod.

"Shadow travel?" Larissa asked.

Loralie nodded again.

"Just don't leave me stuck in the in-between," Larissa ordered.

Loralie set her hand on her shoulder and smiled wide. "You'll be returned safe and sound."

"While you're gone, we'll listen to their radio communications to see if they give anything away. Don't do anything rash or stupid," I said.

Loralie saluted me, and then she and Larissa disappeared.

"She's going to do something stupid, isn't she?" Tsukiko asked with a growl.

I sighed and hung my head. "Probably."

"Frances," Dante whispered behind me.

I turned and looked up into his scowling face. "What?"

"When did you learn to move like that? When did you three learn to coordinate attacks like that?"

"Does that really matter?" I asked him and turned the hand-held radios up a little louder.

"You aren't the same as you were before," he whispered. "You've been hiding things from me."

"Since when does she need to update you on her life?" Tsukiko asked with hands on her hips. "Last time I checked, you two aren't an item. You two haven't even ever been on a date."

"What did you do over the summer?" he asked us both. "What were you three up to?"

"Learning how to protect ourselves," I said. "I don't know if you are aware of this or not, but being from such prestigious monster lines makes us targets not only to humans, but to other monsters as well. You don't know what we have been through. You don't know what I have been through. I don't have to tell you anything."

His mouth dropped open and he blinked at me.

"Night is falling. Prepare for phase two," a female voice said over the radio.

Phase two? What was phase two?

"That doesn't sound good," Tsukiko whispered. "Why aren't Loralie and Larissa back yet?"

They should have been back by now. What was the hold up?

"Come on, Loralie," I whispered nervously. "Hurry up."

Loralie materialized before me, an unconscious Larissa in her arms. "We've got a problem."

A goblin took Larissa and inspected her for wounds.

"She said the barrier is to keep monsters from leaving, not from entering, though. The barrier makes me feel super uncomfortable when I'm near it. Anyway. While we were standing near the barrier, it suddenly thickened and touched her. The barrier's touch knocked her unconscious immediately."

"She's alive," the goblin said. "Just passed out."

"They said they're moving to phase two, but we don't know anything besides that," I informed her.

"I do," she said. "We're going to have to implement Plan Apocalypse."

My mouth dropped and Tsukiko screeched, "What?"

Loralie smiled. "Time to have some fun, besties."

Fun was not what I called Plan Apocalypse. It was draining, dangerous, and would cause everything to change.

Our social lives were about to go out the window.

"Shit," I whispered.

"What's going on?" Dante asked, coming up to my side.

"Don't worry your pretty head," Loralie said and smiled wide. "We're going to save all of you and when we're done, you will either worship or fear us. I'm fine with either."

This was the worst day ever.

CHAPTER 38

TSUKIKO

"You're serious?" I asked Loralie.

She nodded. "We need to get to the other side of the school to take out the magic user who is working with them. Have someone change the barrier to keep everything outside and ensure nothing can come inside. Then, kaboom."

"Kaboom?" Dante asked, scowling.

"Ka. Boom," Loralie said with a wicked smile.

"Who do we know who can change the barrier?" I asked.

"Bogden could," Frances said.

Loralie's smile disappeared. "No."

"He's the strongest and is basically immortal. He is our best option," I argued.

She growled. "There has to be someone else."

"Lor," I whispered.

Her eyes turned red and shadow leaked from her fingertips. "No."

"Stop being a baby," I growled. "He'll be fine."

"What is their plan?" Dante asked. "You said you know what phase two is."

"They're contacting the monster elite to force them to come here. Once all of them are inside the barrier, they're going to kill them in an attempt to summon Lucifer," she said.

My claws shot out of my fingertips, and I growled. They wanted to kill my family. My parents and grandfather. My best friends' parents who were like second and third parents to me. No. I was not going to let that happen.

"What is your plan?" Dante asked.

"You'll just have to wait and see," she said.

"We're going to have to put ourselves in their direct line of sight. They could just shoot us," Frances said.

"We will be fine," Loralie said with a smile. "We can do it. We have done it multiple times before."

"It hurts," I whined. "And feels super weird."

"It's either this or we let our families die," Loralie snapped.

Alright, she got me there.

"Fine, let's go," I growled and set my hand on her arm.

"It sounds like you're planning on killing yourselves," Dante said and grabbed Frances's arm.

"Just a bit, but don't worry, we'll resurrect," Loralie said and pulled Frances out of his hold and into me. She winked at him and then we disappeared into the shadows.

We materialized in a grassy area surrounded by trees and immediately, Bogden rushed over to Loralie. "Are you okay? Why were you gone for so long? Did something happen?"

She swallowed hard. "I'm fine. Look, we need your help."

The three of us explained the situation and what we needed from him. We left out our part of the plan, though.

He nodded. "I can do that."

I tossed one of the handheld radios to a tree nymph who sat in the shade of a nearby tree. "Keep that so you can hear what's going on. Don't freak out when they start talking about getting attacked. That's going to be us. We're going to let you know when we've cleared them out."

She nodded. "Got it."

"Let's check the barrier on this side, since there are fewer guards around," Frances said. "There should be more time between patrols. We'll drop Bogden off and after we leave, he can alter the barrier."

"Is it close enough to walk to?" Loralie asked Bogden. "I'd like to save my power if I can."

He looked up at the sky overhead and then slowly lowered his gaze until it was level with the horizon. "About a five-minute walk."

"Let's go," I ordered and headed in the direction he'd looked. The sooner we got this over with, the better. I wanted to make sure my family was nowhere near the academy when we enacted our plan.

If they saw what we were planning to do, they would ground us for eternity. Or longer.

"Stop scowling, Kiko. Everything is going to be fine," Loralie said with a wide smile. To others, she would have appeared excited and super positive, but I saw the tension in the corners of her eyes, in the way she carried herself, in the rapid pulse on her throat. She was worried, too.

Did she not want to worry Bogden?

That was most likely it.

"I know," I said and forced my ears to perk up. "But you also know I'm a worrier."

"All three of you are," Bogden said as he walked between the three of us. "You take turns acting cool and composed, but all three of you worry constantly about things."

"Do not!" the three of us yelled.

He chuckled. "You totally do."

"You don't understand what it's like for us," Frances whispered.

"I think I understand more than you realize. My mother isn't exactly your run of the mill creature."

That was true. Baba Yaga was a well-known monster who had been hunted for centuries. Humans across all of the countries knew about her.

None of us knew what to say to that, so we finished our walk in silence. There were no humans nearby, so Bogden rushed forward to work on the barrier.

"We're going to go take out the magic user so they can't change the barrier back," Frances informed him. "Stay nearby, but stay hidden. If you need to move to another area, that's fine, but stay close to the barrier. Our plan will only work if you keep the barrier we need intact."

"What is your plan?" He asked.

Loralie fidgeted with her hands a moment and said, "I'm sorry for all the trouble I've caused you this year. Stay safe."

"Why does it sound like you're saying goodbye? Is this a suicide mission? You better not be sacrificing yourselves!"

"We'll take care of the humans," I said. "And each other."

"Loralie," Bogden yelled.

"Bye," she whispered, latched onto Frances and I, and shadow traveled right next to the front of the academy's entrance, mostly hidden by the shadow of the building.

Standing by the entrance was Darla, a witch from an unknown family who came here on a scholarship. She leaned against a pillar, looking out at the road.

"Kill or incapacitate?" Loralie asked.

"Incapacitate," Frances said. "We don't know if she is doing this by force or not."

She didn't look forced to me. She was just standing by the

barrier with arms crossed and kept kicking the dirt with the toe of her boot.

"Fine," Loralie grumbled.

"Plan?" I asked Frances.

"Alright, here's what we're going to do," she said confidently.

I moved to the shadows right behind Darla, popped up, grabbed her, and yanked her down into the shadows with us before she could even open her mouth.

Tsukiko smacked her on the head, knocking her out.

We moved into the nearest building, into an empty classroom, tied her up, and left her there. We weren't sure if she was helping on her own free will or not, so we didn't want to just kill her. We would leave the punishment up to the school.

Step one complete.

Tsukiko's head whipped up as she looked out the window. "My parents are coming. They are still a ways off, but I can feel them getting close."

"Time for Plan Apocalypse," I said and cracked my knuckles. "Showtime, ladies."

We shadow-traveled back to the spot where we had abducted Darla and fully materialized. The three of us stood side by side, facing the school and the humans.

In the front and center was Larson, a dhampir who talked nonstop about escaping the monster world to rule over the humans. He often talked about wanting to make contracts with every human on the earth so he would end up with the largest army in the monster world to take down even Lucifer. We thought he was just talking big to try to seem cool.

Now it all made sense. He had been helping them all along. Had he been the one telling the humans where the monster towns were?

All of the humans raised their weapons and aimed at us.

A woman in the front beside Larson asked, "What are you doing here? How did you get free?"

"What did you think you were going to gain, Larson?" Tsukiko asked. "Why would you betray all of monsterkind and work with humans?"

"You don't understand what it's like for the rest of us. For the low-class monsters of the world. You've all been handed everything you have ever wanted," he hissed at us. He looked at the woman. "Kill them. Kill them now."

With a deep breath, I reached down into the ground, searching with my powers as Death, pulling and pulling bone after bone towards us. It was lucky that there were a few cemeteries nearby.

Tsukiko shifted into her half-shift form and unsheathed her claws.

Frances closed her eyes and whispered her favorite poem to center herself.

"Freeze!" a human yelled. "Whatever you're doing...stop."

"Just kill them!" Larson screamed.

"Stand down," the woman ordered us. "We don't want to hurt any of you."

Once I had enough bones gathered beneath the ground I stood on, I whispered, "Ready."

Frances set a hand on Tsukiko's and my shoulder, and whispered, "Apocalypse."

All three of us linked together spiritually and magically.

The cores of our magic weaved together to create one power being.

The bones I had dug up shot up out of the ground, surrounding us, and formed a giant wolven-raven mutant creature of bones and shadows.

The humans opened fire, but it was too late. The magical shield was already erected to give our creature enough time to fully form around us.

Within its rib cage, we stood together, side by side, and ready to move. I would control replacement of bones if needed, Tsukiko would pilot the creature on fighting instinct, and Frances would strategize and give Tsukiko instructions as needed.

Inside of our creature, we were one.

"What the—" the woman gasped and backed up.

"Do not let them escape," Frances said in an otherworldly voice. "Kill them all."

Tsukiko howled her pleasure and began attacking the nearest humans with our bone claws and the beak that tore through skin like butter.

We couldn't hold this shape for long, so we had to kill them all, as fast as we could.

"Come out humans!" I roared. "Come out and face the reaper."

Ten. Twenty. Thirty humans dead.

Tsukiko took them out without prejudice.

We couldn't fit into the buildings to attack the humans inside.

"Pull them out with our tentacles," Frances ordered.

With concentration, I turned some of the feathers along our back into tentacles, lengthened and thickened them, and sent them into the buildings, dragging the screaming humans out one or two at a time.

As soon as they came out, Tsukiko ended their lives.

"You wanted to see what monsters were like?" Frances asked, her voice projected from our monster. "This is what we are like when hunted. We will destroy every last human who threatens us."

The click of a weapon to our left drew my attention, but we didn't turn fast enough to stop the human from firing a rocket.

It slammed into our creature's flank, knocking us to the side and causing us to slam into the wall.

A hole had been torn and I worked to patch it up with more bones and more feathers and fur and shadows.

Once patched, we killed the human and tossed the weapon out of the barrier so no other could use it against us.

More and more humans came from the buildings, like ants from an anthill.

Some threw grenades while others continued to shoot at us.

Frances's serene face grew furious.

Now was when the real fun started for me.

With a roar, Frances released her control, fully submitting to the wildness inside of her, and allowed our creature free rein to attack.

The sun set and the voices of our family members yelled at us outside of the barrier.

We turned and looked up at the window of the headmistress's office. We would free the teachers to help in case our form gave out before we finished.

A human stood, holding Headmistress Gonzalez by the hair, a knife pressed to her throat. "Stop now, or I will kill her," the human threatened.

"Let us in!" Kenta bellowed outside of the barrier in full warrior mode, drool hanging from his snarling snout.

"Not until we have destroyed them. They mean to kill you. We won't allow the humans to kill our family and friends. We will slaughter every last one first," our creature said. No longer were we separate. Now, we were completely joined as one.

"Let us in!" Albus yelled.

Baba Yaga stepped forward and placed her hand on the barrier. "My son is controlling this. That little twerp. It's going to take me a second to break this."

"Last warning," the human holding the headmistress threatened.

With careful movements, we sent a tentacle up the side of the wall, hidden thanks to the shadows of the night. Just as it reached the windowsill, we used a bone shard to become the tip and thrust it up into the human's head.

We were merging more.

Quickly. We had to finish this quickly.

If we didn't separate into...

Who were we before we were us?

Headmistress Gonzalez shoved the dead human out the window.

"Girls, you need to separate," a female voice said from the other side of the barrier.

Turning, we faced the monsters outside the barrier. They were all powerful and looked very angry.

Enemies?

"You would fight us?" we asked.

"Separate," the large, snarling wolfman said.

We snarled and the feathers on our back bristled and shook in anger. "We do not take orders from you. Or anyone." Our tentacles danced in the air above us, waiting to be used against anyone else who opposed us.

Young monsters started coming out of the buildings, their eyes fixed on us.

Yes.

Fear us.

Examine us.

Worship us.

The barrier disappeared and the monsters charged in.

The wolfman tried to grab our neck, but we dodged and sent him flying across the yard with a tentacle.

With concentration, we added bone spikes to all of our tentacles.

A dark man with shadow powers and a huge scythe swung at us.

We easily deflected the blade and hit him with the back of our claw, making him stumble back into some of the other monsters.

A black-winged man, beautiful and terrifying, appeared between the monsters and us. He looked up at us and smiled. "Magnificent."

"They won't separate," one of the female monsters said.

"We will not be defeated!" we roared. "We take orders from no one!"

The black-winged man's eyes narrowed, and he flared his wings out. "You will separate and you will take orders from me, children. I am Lucifer, your ruler, and I will not allow insubordination. Now, separate!"

We snarled. "No."

His eyes turned wholly black, a strange dark light emitted from him, and his fury became palpable.

We tensed, waiting for his attack, but it did not come.

With a deep sigh, he relaxed, folded his wings in, and said, "You need to learn your limits, girls." With a single jump, he smacked us on the back of our head with the side of his hand, and that one hit knocked us unconscious.

CHAPTER 40

LORALIE

Lucifer stayed until we woke up, then gathered Frances, Tsukiko, and I into a small room used for scolding monsters who broke the rules.

Our family had tried to come, but he had ordered them to stay out.

The three of us fidgeted in the really uncomfortable chairs as he continued to stare at us in silence. It had been four minutes already and he hadn't said a word.

I kept opening my mouth to say something, but Frances squeezed my hand each time to keep me silent. I hated tense silence.

After another minute, he leaned back, set his hands in his lap, and said, "You three have a very interesting bond."

We waited for him to say more, but he didn't. Were the long silences meant to be torture for me? Did he know I hated this?

"We know it isn't normal for monsters to have a bond like this," Frances said. "We did not intentionally create the bond."

"It just sort of...happened," Tsukiko said.

"Are we in trouble?" I blurted. "We saved everyone with

minimal damage to the school, so I don't understand why we are in trouble."

His lip twitched. "You did save everyone. You also attacked your family because of how much you merged. Although, you should have been able to recognize your family members with your combined memories. Did you merge with another monster, too?"

"We only attacked them because they attacked us," I countered.

Normally, we had no memory of our time in that form, but we remembered everything this time. Frances couldn't figure out why it was different and it was seriously bothering her.

"Did you merge with another monster, too?" he asked again, his face serious.

"Sort of," Frances whispered. "We don't really know what happened, but ever since the summer, we have been more drawn to someone. Someone different for each of us. I'm not sure if that's what has caused our merging to be different this time. We have tried to ignore the draw, but..."

His lip twitched as he fought back a smile. "I see. Do they know?"

"No," I said with a sigh. "We know things wouldn't work with them, so we have been trying to push them away." Not very successfully.

"Not that that's been possible," Tsukiko growled.

"Why wouldn't it work?" Lucifer asked.

My cheeks warmed, and I saw the other two blush as well.

"It's different for each of us," I whispered.

He put his elbows on the table and leaned his chin on his fists. "I've got all the time in the world, girls. Tell me all about it."

We took turns explaining our situations and our stances. Once we started going, it all tumbled out.

Had he used magic on us? Or was it because he was just naturally easy to talk to?

Once we finished, he leaned back, tilted his head to look up at the ceiling, and burst into laughter so loud it made Tsukiko cringe.

He laughed until tears came from his eyes and he had to wipe them away. "I'm sorry, girls. I'm not laughing at you. Well, sort of. I'm more laughing at this situation. This is all stuff I hadn't expected to happen anytime this millennia."

"What is it?" I asked.

"You understand the witches have Selene, who is the three lunar witches combined into one being?"

We nodded.

"You three are like that, but sort of reversed. You are the three monsters who can combine to form a new monster."

"What is this monster?" Tsukiko asked.

"I call it Cerberus, named after the Greek mythology about a three headed dog, but it tells us a new name it wants to be called each time it is reincarnated," he said. "Normally, it is created with three monsters of the same type, but your strong connection is likely the cause for you being chosen."

"What does this have to do with the males?" Tsukiko asked.

"I'm getting there," he said, but his tone was playful still. "Cerberus and the three who combined to make him needed a conduit because of how powerful they were. So, they latched onto the nearest, most compatible mates who could help them distribute the magic easily and were capable of protecting them from those who wished to destroy them."

"Come again?" I wheezed.

He smiled. "Your magic chose them."

"What if we don't want them?" Frances asked.

His smile softened. "Your fears are understood, but they will diminish over time."

This was insane.

"So, the three of us are powerful monsters who can combine to become Cerberus and because we are so powerful, we needed additional conduits. We latched onto the ones who were nearest us and who could help channel the power and protect us?" Frances asked.

"Exactly," Lucifer said.

"Does it usually happen to monsters as young as us?" I asked.

He shook his head. "No, which is another abnormality for this reincarnation. Though, I'm not really surprised. Cerberus likes to keep us on our toes each time. Last time it was half-octopus and terrorized the oceans, destroying pirate and navy ships alike."

"So, when it is reincarnated, it uses animals compatible with the monster it is merging with?" I asked. "Hence our bird and wolf hybrid?"

He nodded and smiled. "You three are bright. I'm glad I don't have to explain much. The last trio was rather stupid and that was likely why they didn't last long. I warned them not to mess with the humans so much, but they were cocky."

"Why does this being even exist?" Frances asked. "What is the point of such a strong monster?"

Lucifer shrugged, his shoulders and wings moving up and down with the movement. "Don't ask me. I didn't create it. I just found it. Well, it found me and attacked me. We've had a few fights since then. I'm glad you are young and new to the power or I might have had to hurt you. I don't like beating up kids, so it would have left a bad taste in my mouth."

"How kind of you," Tsukiko whispered under her breath.

"Did you find out who was helping the humans?" I asked.

He scowled and nodded. "There were some dhampirs and vampires who thought the humans could help them start a business in the human world. They planned to add some verbiage in their contracts that forced the humans to give their souls to them. Honestly, that was pretty smart and I'm really mad I didn't think of it. However, the humans were planning to double cross them anyway. Plus, I would have found out eventually and punished them. They are being punished currently."

I didn't even want to think about the type of punishment they could be receiving.

"And the potion they used on us?" Frances asked.

"Manufactured by a coven of witches that had been captured. We believe that is the main reason that Darla helped them with creating the barrier. They were testing it on the villages that were destroyed. They tested it and then killed the creatures and burned them so we wouldn't find out. We had some Seers show us the past so we could see what they were really doing while there. We have erased all records of the potion as well as any human who had knowledge of it," he answered.

"You're sure no human will have record or knowledge of it?" I asked.

He smiled. "I can never be one hundred percent certain, but we will deal with it if we find some. We have spies in many areas throughout the human world. Though, it troubles me that this group of humans flew under my radar for so long. Perhaps I need to re-incentivize my operatives."

All three of us tensed.

I was very glad I wasn't one of his operatives.

Lucifer stood and said, "So, you three are going to wait here until I return. When I return, it will be to collect you so you can join your families. I will explain the situation to them so they don't bombard you with too many questions you aren't sure how to answer. Okay?"

We nodded.

"I'll have some food brought for you, too. Tsukiko is looking a little hungry," he said, winked, and left the room.

"This is..." Frances started, but trailed off.

"Unbelievable," Tsukiko said. "Even by monster standards."

And that was saying something.

CHAPTER 41

FRANCES

Lucifer left us in the room for thirty minutes. In that time, a super submissive werewolf we'd never seen before brought us food before scurrying out like she thought we might devour her instead of the food she brought.

"So, what are we supposed to do with this information?" Loralie asked as she shoved a bread roll in her mouth.

"It certainly explains a few things," I whispered. "And yet I still have a ton of questions."

"You always have questions," Tsukiko mumbled around the meat in her mouth.

I stuck my tongue out at her.

She wasn't wrong, so I couldn't argue.

"How do you think the guys are going to take this?" Loralie asked, setting the piece of fruit in her hand back down on the table.

I reached over and squeezed her hand. "It's going to be okay. We have each other."

Tsukiko set her hand on top of mine and nodded. "We will face whatever lay before us together."

Lucifer opened the door and cheerily said, "Follow me, Monsterettes."

We shared a look, took a collective breath, and followed Lucifer down the hallway to the headmistress's office.

Inside the office, Tsukiko, Loralie, and my families sat on couches facing Bogden, Dante, and Rathik's families. Headmistress Gonzalez sat at her desk, her fingers interlocked and her chin resting atop them. No one looked happy.

Standing in front of their families were Dante, Rathik, and Bogden. They were staring at the floor, but their bodies tensed when we walked in.

Lucifer pointed at the carpet in front of our families. "Stand there, please."

We did. Only a fool disobeyed Lucifer.

He stood between the boys and us, smiling happily. "Everyone has been apprised of the situation. I understand that this is not what you may have planned for your child's future, but this is not something that can be altered."

"Except by death," Baba Yaga muttered.

"Say that again, I dare you," Kenta said, his lips pulled back in a snarl.

"Enough," Lucifer snapped. "Do not make me issue punishments because you're being childish."

Loralie reached over and grabbed my hand, her pulse raced so hard I could feel it through her hand.

I understood her fear. She had unintentionally bound Baba Yaga's only son as her future mate. Baba Yaga was not someone you wanted to have as an enemy.

"We didn't choose this," I said, surprised and thankful that my voice came out strong instead of shaky.

"We know," Mom said behind me. "No one is blaming you, Frances."

Doctor Frankenstein burst into the room, her eyes wide and mouth open. "I need to observe them!"

Lucifer sighed, ran his hand down his face, and asked, "How did you find out?"

She scoffed. "Like word of monsters merging wouldn't be spread like wildfire by gossip." With a fast spin, she turned to face us, then set her hands on each of my cheeks. "I always knew you were special. You are my greatest creation."

"Hey!" Dad snapped.

She ignored him. "We might need to upgrade your parts. You already popped a stitch because of the wear and tear you recklessly cause. I'm not sure how much magic your body will be able to channel."

"You can talk to them later. We are having a serious discussion," Lucifer said.

She pouted. "Luci, you're so mean."

Luci? Had she really just referred to the ruler of the Underworld as "Luci"?

He pointed at the door she'd left open.

After stomping her foot like an angry child, she walked out and closed the doors behind her.

Lucifer ran his hand down his face while muttering in another language, recomposed himself, and raised his head. "Okay. So, here we go. Everyone knows what's happened and their parts in this situation. Now, let's hear from anyone who wants to speak."

Baba Yaga opened her mouth.

He interrupted her. "No threats or suggestions of killing any of the six children or I will have a private chat with you later."

She closed her mouth.

"We're sorry we dragged you into this," Tsukiko whispered to the guys. "We didn't do it on purpose. If there's a way to separate you from us, we'll try to find one."

"There isn't," Lucifer said.

"They don't have to stay near us, right?" Loralie asked Lucifer. "They could go on with their lives and—"

"We don't want that," Bogden said, interrupting her.

"You haven't even asked how we felt," Rathik said. "You just started apologizing. Though, that is pretty typical for you three."

"They always assume the worst," Dante said.

"How do you feel?" I asked, a lump forming in my throat.

"Did any of you open your gifts from us?" Dante asked, folding his arms across his chest.

We all looked down. I shook my head and saw Loralie and Tsukiko do the same out of the corner of my eye.

"Did you throw them away?" Rathik asked.

"No," Tsukiko said. "We just put them in a box."

"In the closet," Loralie added.

"Girls!" Sakura gasped. "Why would you do such a thing?"

"I swear, there has to be someone doing this to us just to torment us," Loralie whispered.

"What do you mean?" Loralie's mom asked.

"Terrified of fire," Loralie said and pointed at me. She pointed at Dante. "Phoenix." She pointed at Tsukiko. "Terrified of snakes." She pointed at Rathik. "Naga." Her hand dropped.

"Immortal," Tsukiko said and pointed at Bogden. "Death," she said and pointed at Loralie.

Loralie's eyes narrowed at Tsukiko, but Tsukiko just smiled at her.

There was silence in the room for a heartbeat or two. Then, every single adult burst into belly-clutching, tears-streaming laughter.

CHAPTER 42

I couldn't remember the last time I had seen our families laugh so hard.

The fact that it was about something serious regarding us really irked me.

Growling, I snapped, "I'm glad this is so funny for you."

Grandfather wiped his eyes and said, "Child, we are not laughing at you."

"A little bit," Dad said.

"We are laughing at the irony and the humor in the situation. You three bound yourselves to males who embody your worst fears," Grandfather finished.

"It's not funny," Frances said, folded her arms across her chest, and dropped her head.

She was about two seconds from crying.

I reached towards her hand to grab it, but Dante walked forward and distracted me.

He squatted down so he could look up at her face. "We were touching most of today, remember? Did I burn you? Were you hyperventilating?"

She sniffled. "No."

"You were doing what most of the day?" Frances's dad asked.

"What if in the future, we decide to have a kid?" Frances asked.

"Over my dead body," Frances's dad growled.

"You're already dead," Dante's dad said with a wide smile. He was a handsome phoenix with almost white flames for hair. The amount of power he had in order to have his hair made of flames that were so high in temperature was mind boggling.

"What if the baby goes phoenix and I drop it?" Frances finished.

"You're infertile," Dr. Frankenstein said from outside the door.

Lucifer groaned and dropped his head while shaking it. "That human is such a pain in my feathers. Doc, you might as well come in since you're already eavesdropping."

"Gathering intel," she corrected as she came back inside.

"I'm...what?" Frances asked.

"Your parents had me make you, remember?" Dr. Frankenstein asked, her tone the most gentle I had ever heard it.

Who knew the doc had a bedside manner?

"So, it won't be a problem, but that makes another problem," Frances said and looked at Dante.

Dante smiled. "It's not a problem. If, in the distant future, we decide we want a child, we could adopt or something."

"We could always make one," Dr. Frankenstein said, her eyes bright and smile almost splitting her face in half. "I'd love to try to make a phoenix hybrid."

"Had you asked us, instead of assuming the worst, we would have told you that we are fine with this. We have been trying to convince you three to date us all year and besides, you didn't do this out of malice," Bogden said.

I looked at Rathik, my tail in my hands to keep it from

twitching behind me. I tried to keep my ears up, too, but they drooped no matter how hard I tried. "You've been rather quiet. Do you really feel the same? I'm not infertile, though I'm not sure we could crossbreed anyway since our races are so different." I asked him.

"Oh, you totally can," Dr. Frankenstein said. "I've seen them."

"Them?" I asked, my eyes widening. I glanced at my parents, but they were staring at Dr. Frankenstein like they could make her explode just from their glares alone.

Lucifer snarled. "What have you been doing in the Sahara Desert, Doc?"

She blanched. "Uh..."

"We can take precautions to prevent that," Rathik said and shrugged. "I'm not too worried about it. Hopefully, by then, you'll be a little more over your fear of snakes."

This was really happening? They were really okay with being tied to us?

"Wait," Frances gasped. "If we are all tied together and Bogden and Loralie are immortal, does that mean—"

Lucifer beamed like a proud parent. "I told you they were smart! Yes, it seems the reincarnation cycle has ended."

Baba Yaga moaned and then fainted on the couch, her head falling over into Rathik's mother's lap.

Everyone stared in silence.

"Frances, I think you should get an award or something," Dad whispered. "You're the first person in history to make Baba Yaga faint."

The room erupted in laughter once again, but this time it was something we could join in on.

Life returned to normal, or as normal as a monster academy could be. The guys declared themselves our boyfriends and took their jobs as our protectors very seriously.

Some students were scared of us, but most treated us like Ainsley did. She asked a billion questions and kept trying to convince us to merge again.

Lucifer gave us strict orders not to merge unless it was an absolute emergency, though.

He had also smacked the backs of our heads when he learned that we were trying to protect not only our families, but him as well. "I am perfectly capable of protecting myself from some humans," he'd snarled.

We knew he was right, but at the time we weren't really thinking about how strong he was.

The next months passed quickly and before we knew it, the prom was upon us. We'd been lectured because we had skipped so many planning meetings, but offered to spend a ton of our free time decorating for it. We did feel bad that we had ended up only attending one meeting, so we did a ton of work preparing and gathering everything we needed for decorating.

Ainsley twirled in front of the mirror, her bright pink dress had a tattered hem and showed off her color matching freshly painted talons. It had taken her an hour just to curl her hair, but it looked gorgeous and bounced as she moved. "Tonight, is going to be amazing," she squealed.

I smiled and pulled my tail through the slit in my dress. "I'm actually looking forward to a dance for the first time in my life," I said.

She rolled her eyes. "That's because you have the hottest guys in the school for dates. I need to find some new wing women or I might be single forever."

Loralie pulled her black lace gloves on and then patted

Ainsley on the head. "You'll find the right male for you, Ainsley. I can feel it."

"Don't you usually just sense death?" she asked, her mouth open in horror.

Loralie smacked her arm, and Ainsley cackled before returning to examine her makeup one more time.

Frances brushed down some of my tail's fur. "Let me help."

"Thanks," I said with a smile in the mirror. "It's hard to see it well."

"Ready?" Loralie asked from the door.

She wore a black dress that hugged her curves, had a corset around the waist, and tied up in the back with bright purple laces. Her lace gloves and fishnet stockings completed the look.

I checked my reflection, adjusting my hair around my ears before nodding. "Yep."

The four of us walked with wide smiles out of the dorms and to the multipurpose room in subfloor five where all events were held.

We had spent two days decorating the room for our Heaven and Hell theme. Instead of the usual splitting of top and bottom for heaven and hell, we had split the room in half. One half of the room was decorated in dark purple and black with red flames in small pits lined with skulls. The other half of the room was decorated in white and gold with some splashes of red to commemorate the angels who had been slain by Lucifer.

We had gotten Lucifer's approval for the theme first, of course. To our surprise, he had been thrilled with the idea.

Lucifer sat on a throne of papier-mâché bones and wood crates designed specifically for him, in a beautiful half white and half black suit, and smiled as he watched the students dancing before him.

We waved to him as we headed to the center of the room, not wanting to stand in the doorway and block it.

He waved back and resumed watching everyone else while tapping his foot along to the beat of the music.

There were several parent chaperones and much to my dismay, my parents were among them. As was my grandfather who I could see dancing with my grandmother.

Were chaperones allowed to dance? Not that anyone would likely tell my grandparents to stop, or that they would listen.

"Where are they?" Frances asked, fidgeting with the flame pendant necklace Dante had given her.

We had all finally opened our gifts from them and found that they were gifts that related to them specifically with a note asking about starting to date. Mine had been a pendant with one of Rathik's scales encased in resin. Loralie's had been a ring shaped like a raven with the wings wrapped around her finger.

The guys denied it, but we were certain they had gotten together to plan out the gifts.

"They said they would meet us here, right?" Frances asked.

I set my hand on her shoulder. "Relax, they'll be here."

"Who will?" Rathik asked behind me.

The three of us spun around and in sync, our mouths dropped.

Rathik had on a dark green suit that reminded me of his scales and had his hair slicked back. I didn't think I'd ever seen him look so handsome.

"You expecting someone else?" Dante asked. His suit was a burnt orange and the flames of his hair were low and shaped like spikes, glowing a neon blue.

"You look beautiful," Bogden told Loralie, holding out a black orchid corsage.

"You look really good in a suit," I whispered and then wished I could take the words back.

Rathik smiled wide and kissed my cheek. "Thank you. You look gorgeous, as always."

"Care to dance?" Dante asked and held out a bent arm to Frances.

She nodded, gulped, and then slid a shaky hand into the crook of his elbow.

"Milady?" Rathik asked, bowed, and held out a hand, palm up.

I set my hand in it and curtsied. "Milord."

"Nerds," Loralie whispered behind us.

Rathik spun me out into the middle of the dance floor and I was certain I didn't stop smiling the entire night and well into the next morning.

Life wasn't perfect. There were still a lot of unknowns and uncertainties in our futures, but as long as we had each other, I knew we could make it through anything.

Friendship and love were what united us. No matter what the humans thought, even monsters felt those emotions and we cherished them just as much. We would kill anyone or anything that threatened our family and friends. With teeth, claws, and magic.

Until the end of time.

Baba Yaga glared at Loralie while Loralie's father glared at Bogden. Dad glared at Dante and wouldn't stop no matter how many times I kicked him beneath the table.

Lucifer sat at the head of the table, smiling wide as he sipped from a wine glass. The liquid was dark, but the consistency made me think it wasn't actually wine.

"This has to be the most tense dinner I've ever been to," Loralie whispered to me, leaning close so we wouldn't be overheard.

"Which is saying something because we have been to some crazy dinners," I whispered back.

Loralie chuckled and nodded.

As long as I could get her to relax, everything would be alright.

Sakura glided in wearing a red and gold dress that put everything I owned to shame. "Sorry I am late. Things got a little complicated during a meeting and I had to calm everyone down."

Looking a bit closer, I noticed some of the red on her dress was stained, most likely dried blood.

As soon as she sat, Lucifer set his glass down. "I brought you here to discuss how I would like to proceed with the children."

"What?" Baba Yaga and my mother shrieked.

"What do you mean proceed?" I asked, swallowing past the lump now in my throat.

Loralie reached over, grabbing my hand with hers.

"It is important that you be properly trained in regards to your Cerberus powers," Lucifer said. "As well as with the powers that come from being joined with the males."

"We have been training," Loralie said quickly.

We had. Every weekend, we spent half a day working on our powers and figuring out the proper way to channel the magic through the guys.

"You six are going to be very important to monsterkind," Lucifer continued. "That is why you are now going to spend your holiday and summer breaks with me."

"You?" Sakura spluttered.

Never in my life had I seen her react in such a way.

Lucifer smiled. "Yes. They will be our greatest weapon, and as such, I am personally going to train them."

Personally trained by Lucifer? It was something every monster wished for. Many would even kill for the chance.

"As their parents, you will be permitted to visit them, but they need to focus and you will only cause them stress," he continued.

"We do not cause them stress," Baba Yaga said and folded her arms over her chest.

"This is the most stressful dinner I've been to since the aliens visited," Lucifer scoffed.

Aliens?

"Nonetheless, this is my decision and it will start this summer. Any objections?"

No one spoke.

He beamed. "Wonderful. Now, let's eat."

Monster Academy was hard enough. Could I handle being trained by Lucifer?

Loralie squeezed my hand. "Together."

I nodded. Right. Together we could make it through everything.

"Together," Tsukiko whispered on Loralie's other side.

I nodded, squeezed Loralie's hand, and smiled at Dante.

It had been one hell of a year at Monster Academy, but with my friends at my side, the future would be a piece of chocolate and stardust cake.

ACKNOWLEDGMENTS

There are so many that deserve acknowledgments and I am certain I am going to miss some of them. So, I apologize in advance.

Thank you to Crescent Sea Publishing for taking a chance on me.

KM, thank you for being supportive and guiding me with this project.

Avery, your support and love are what continues to drive me.

RJ, Erin, and Jennifer L. are always there to help me when I'm stuck, give me advice, talk things out, and provide me the type of support I hope every author has. You three are phenomenal and I don't know if I can ever express how much you mean to me.

KD, thank you for creating such a gorgeous cover! You are a treasure.

Ericka, your support means the world to me. Your support, feedback, and excitement have gotten me through some dark days.

Pauline, my amazing editor, you are exceptional and I love working with you.

Finally, thank you to every person reading this book. Thank you for giving my writing a chance. I hope you enjoyed it and I hope you try other books I have written.

ABOUT THE AUTHOR

Catherine Banks is a USA Today bestselling fantasy author who writes in several fantasy subgenres and has multiple pseudonyms. She began writing fiction at only four years old and finished her first full-length novel at the age of fifteen. She is married to her soulmate and best friend, Avery, who she has two amazing children with. After her full-time job, she reads books, plays video games, and watches anime shows and movies with her family to relax. Although she has lived in Northern California her entire life, she dreams of traveling around the world. Catherine is also C.E.O. of Turbo Kitten Industries™, a company with many hats including being a book publisher and Etsy store full of nerdy fun.

facebook.com/catherinebanksauthor

twitter.com/catherineebanks

amazon.com/author/catherinebanks

bookbub.com/authors/catherine-banks

MORE BOOKS YOU'LL LOVE

If you enjoyed Monster Academy, please consider leaving a review!

Then check out more books from Catherine Banks and Crescent Sea Publishing!

THE SIREN WARS BY K.M. ROBINSON

War has hovered around the kingdom of Scylla for generations ever since the original sirens left the mer collection generations ago after nearly drowning the human prince. Over the years, select mermaids from the royal bloodline have been trained as spies to work for the reigning kings and queens, keeping the collection safe from sirens and humans.

Celena and her partner, Merrick, work covertly for the royals—not even her twin brother knows. When they discover the sirens have broken through the barriers the mer set up to keep the sirens out, Celena and her friends must race to the old kingdom of Metten to stop them from starting a war within their borders.

When she's dragged to the surface, Celena realizes that the war above the waters is as deadly as the one below the waves—and sacrificing herself may be the only way to protect her family.

The Siren Wars have only just begun.

Now available from Crescent Sea Publishing!
sirenwars.crescentseapublishing.com

If you were thrown into a war between a Fae clan and a witch coven, would you be able to uncover the truth before the stroke of Midnight?

Nova Kramer blames herself for the death of her mother and sister—so does her father. When he moves them to Danville City to escape the reminders of what they lost, Nova is thrown right back into a world full of anxiety when their new neighbor, Stella, and her twin brothers make it their mission to bring Nova to her knees—after all, they know her secret—and blackmail is just the start.

Kent Danville and his brothers have a secret, too—their clan is working to take down a coven of witches and find the other five clans of Fae, but when Nova walks into his life, the Fae can't seem to stop thinking about her. He can't risk falling for the new girl—he has a soulmate out there somewhere, and a mission to complete...if the coven doesn't kill him first.

A war is brewing between the coven and the clan—each side a little less human than the other—and Nova may get caught in the crossfire if she can't discover the truth before the clock strikes Midnight.

Now available from Crescent Sea Publishing!
midnight.crescentseapublishing.com

Calvin's Alien Adventure

Artemis Lupine Series
Song of the Moon
Kiss of a Star
Healed by the Fire
Battles of the Night
Artemis Lupine, The Complete Series

Pirate Princess Trilogy
Pirate Princess
Princess Triumvirate
Pirate Queen*

Little Death Bringer Duology
Mercenary
Protector
Little Death Bringer, The Official Coloring Book

Her Royal Harem Series
Royally Entangled
Royally Exposed
Royally Elected
Royally Enraged
Her Royal Harem, The Complete Series
The Demon's Fair
Her Royal Harem, The Coloring Book

Zodiac Shifters Paranormal Romance Series
Centaur's Prize
Tiger Tears
Lion About

The Lioness's Harem Trilogy
Lonely Lioness
Leery Lioness*

Anderelle: Minloa Trilogy
Queen of the Stars
Empress of the Galaxy
Goddess of the Universe

Bonds of Madness Series
Sealing the Deal
Spilling the Beans*

Ciara Steele Novella Series
True Faces
Barbaric Tendencies

Monster Academy

Demonic Contract

Anja's Secret

Daughter of Lions

Dragon's Blood

The Last Werewolf

Last Ama Princess

Transforming Rose

Lady Serra and the Draconian

Alys of Asgard

Phoenix Possessed

Sybil Deceived

The Pawn

Stone Heart

Of Sky and Sea

COMING SOON

www.ingramcontent.com/pod-product-compliance
Lightning Source LLC
Chambersburg PA
CBHW032103180726
48284CB00002B/425